BLACK ICE

A StormWatch Novel

REGAN BLACK

Getaway Reads, LLC

BLACK ICE

Print Edition ISBN: 9781705949825

Cover Design by VK Hinze
Published by Getaway Reads, LLC in the United States of America

DEDICATION

With special thanks to Deb, Vicki, Peggy, Rita, and Cindy. It's an honor and joy to work with each of you—authors I'm delighted to count as both inspiring mentors and wonderful friends.

DEADWOOD 5 NEWS

"Good evening. I'm Joyce Adams for Channel Five Weather. The National Weather Service has just released an updated warning for our area for winter storm Holly. The outlook here in Deadwood is not improving.

"After inundating Nebraska with record accumulations, Holly is determined to keep snow plows and salt trucks in business here in South Dakota. Previous predictions that we should expect two to four feet of snow have been increased to six to eight feet in some areas. Drifts to ten or twelve feet are possible, with the high winds associated with Holly.

"If those numbers sound impossible, that's because we haven't seen a storm like this in eighty years. Now is the time to check your emergency supplies. You can find a list at our website, or use the ticker at the bottom of your screen. Please, double check your emergency plans and be prepared for road closures as early as tomorrow morning.

"Trooper Bob, our correspondent from the South Dakota Highway Patrol, has more information. Over to you, Trooper Bob."

CHAPTER ONE

Deadwood, South Dakota

With her laptop perched on her knees and ear buds in her ears, Evelyn Cotton hit refresh, hoping this time the man she was scheduled to chat with would be in the online meeting room. Thanks to technology, it was her first face-to-face meeting with a potential investor in the family business she was trying to save.

Except he wasn't showing up and she couldn't sit here staring at the screen forever. She had to get over to the casino for her evening shift. This time of year, wild winter storms or not, dealing poker at the Silver Aces kept this family in the black.

Barely.

The investor, Tate Cordell, had contacted Cottonwood Adventures a few weeks ago. They'd hit it off over the phone and he'd requested a personal tour to get a feel for the area and a better idea of her plans to expand and offer winter activities. She was happy to oblige, but he'd cancelled last week's visit at the last moment, after she'd traded away her shift. With the sudden weather system jacking up flights and travel plans, they'd opted for an online meeting.

"Come on, Tate."

"He called?" her father, Dale, half-shouted from his beloved recliner. He'd spent the day in his woodshop, restoring a set of kitchen chairs for a friend.

"No." She shook her head. "Must be trouble with the connection."

"Or he lost interest."

Gee thanks. Evelyn suppressed a scathing glare. It was bad enough sitting here as if she'd been stood up by a date. "He'll call." She reached for her boots and pulled them on. When he *did* show—and he *would*—she wanted to make the most of every remaining minute.

"Then what's with the boots?"

She forcibly reminded herself that her dad loved her, even when he didn't show it in normal ways or even in ways she might prefer. Plus, big storms like the one closing in on them usually amped up his depression issues. "There's no sense wrecking my good shoes crossing the parking lot," she replied. If the meeting with Tate went well, this might be her last winter at the casino. Her heart actually fluttered at the happy thought.

For several seasons now, her father had posed significant resistance to her many suggestions and ideas that would shift Cottonwood from merely scraping by as an average three-season tour operation to a thriving year-round profitable endeavor. Whether or not he believed she could do it, he seemed determined to prevent her from trying. None of her spreadsheets or marketing plans had changed his mind. All she needed to put them on the map was a modest financial investment for new gear, a storage building, a website overhaul and a couple of new hires. *All* sounded like a lot, but she knew how to prioritize and make every penny stretch.

Her father, despite the evidence in the roof over his head and food on the table, wasn't convinced of her ability. Every time she asked, Dale refused to even consider a business loan, leaving Evelyn to get creative.

"I wish you'd stay home." He pointed at the television, where another aspiring journalist was bundled up against the gusting wind and blowing snow. "It's going to get worse in a hurry."

"It's a wonder the mic doesn't freeze over," she muttered. Her laptop chimed and she scrambled back in front of the camera, only to see that the meeting had timed out without starting. The chime was an email alert from the casino. Small comfort to know the internet connection was fine on her end. "Damn."

Her father snorted, either agreeing with her assessment or disapproving of her vocabulary. It didn't matter. She and Dale hadn't seen eye to eye on much of anything since her mother, Tess, died during Evelyn's senior year of college.

"Only goes to show you shouldn't be out in this mess," he said.

"I wish it was as easy as calling in," she said. "My boss just asked me to confirm I can make tonight's shift and she's hoping I'll stick around to work through the storm."

"You told me they were evacuating the resorts."

"Dad." Evelyn clung to her last scrap of patience as she turned off her laptop and stowed it away. Tate would reschedule. It helped to remember that he wasn't the only backup plan she had working. "They were discussing the option. If people can't get out of town, they'll need entertainment." She'd packed an overnight bag and stowed it in her car, just in case the roads were impassable and she had to stay over.

"You're risking your neck just so they won't miss a dollar," he grumbled when she crossed the room to tell him goodbye.

She could launch into a lecture about the economic boost the casinos brought to Deadwood with events and tourism every single month. The Silver Aces even recommended Cottonwood Adventures to guests when the company was open. She could mention how the casinos reinvested a generous chunk of their profits back to the community year after year. She could, but she'd be wasting her breath.

"There's meatloaf in the fridge when you're ready." She wrapped her scarf around her neck and kissed her dad's graying hair before shrugging into her coat. Grabbing her overnight bag, she escaped her well-meaning father and headed for her car.

Between the wind and the temperature drop, the air had more bite as she stepped outside. She leaned into the wind, averting her face and wishing she'd parked in the garage. Thankfully, her compact SUV started right up with the same dependability it had shown for years. She turned on her radio for some upbeat music to perk up for her shift. Tate being a no show was a bummer, but dwelling on that disappointment would negatively impact her tips. Unfortunately, her favorite station was in full storm-mode.

"People." Winter Storm Holly was becoming a local obsession. She navigated the winding driveway from her life-long home, past the turn off for the Cottonwood Adventures office and to the main road. "It's not our first brush with snow." She laughed at herself, eyeing the remains of the most recent snowfall lining the shoulders on either side of the road and covering the wilderness in a blanket of white.

Traffic was lighter than she expected and, once she was out of the driveway, the roads were mostly clear. Though she'd lived here all her life, it was hard even for her to imagine six feet of snow at the minimum. Maybe people were being smart and heeding the warnings to prepare for the worst. While that was the smart and safe way to go, it could cost her on a night when she needed the tips.

She was almost to the casino before she found a station still playing pop remakes of Christmas classics. It was enough to put a smile on her face as she finished the drive and circled for the closest parking space she could find.

As she gathered her purse and the bag with her good shoes, her cell phone rang. "Come on, Dad," she groaned. But she brightened when the screen showed Tate Cordell's number. Sucking in a quick breath, she pulled off her glove and swiped the screen to answer. "Cottonwood Adventures, Evelyn speaking."

"Evelyn!" He sounded slightly out of breath. "I am so, so sorry I didn't make our appointment."

She stopped herself before she spewed platitudes and nonsense that he shouldn't worry about it. It was time to change tactics. She'd been far too accessible in their prior conversations. He was a busy man, but she was no slouch.

"I hope everything is well," she said neutrally. "I'm about to head into another meeting." It wasn't a lie, she'd be meeting plenty of people on her shift. And she did need to speak with the manager on the hospitality side of the casino operations about her recent proposal for team-building excursions and events. "Please, send me an email and we can reschedule. Have a great—"

"Hang on." His tone hardened. "My internet connection went out."

"I hate it when that happens," she sympathized. The weather was already draining the warm air from the car. Her ungloved hand was getting chilled. "Whenever it's back up and running, send that email."

"You promised me a tour of the area."

Her cold fingers were quickly forgotten. He still planned

to visit? He'd agreed to her outrageous price of a thousand dollars for a glorified walk through the woods, despite it being a snow-heavy season. They'd scheduled for the day after tomorrow and she'd assumed, especially after he didn't make the online meeting that he'd intended to delay the entire thing. "You're in Deadwood?"

"Almost," he replied. "Travel is interesting at best, but yes, I changed my plans to get ahead of the storm."

"Holly is a beast," she agreed as a gust sent snow swirling across her windshield. "And I'm afraid the last update said the storm was barreling straight for us. We really should postpone until the worst has passed."

"If I can get in tonight?"

His tenacity, the press in his voice, surprised her. "I'm not available until tomorrow at the earliest." Maybe not then if she had to cover for a coworker.

"What do you recommend?"

"With this storm?" She looked up at the heavy gray sky, gloomier still as evening deepened and the light faded. "I recommend you wait it out. The wilderness will still be here once Holly blows over and everyone can dig out."

"Dig out?"

She hadn't asked, but she got the impression Tate had been raised in a warm climate. "They're predicting several feet of snow accumulation. Factor in the drifts and it could be difficult if not impossible to get around for a few days."

"I didn't realize."

Loosely translated into business-speak, that meant she wouldn't be getting an influx of cash anytime soon. Worse, she might have just botched the deal, giving him the impression this was winter every year. She scrambled to salvage something from the call. "A winter storm like this one isn't something we see often, not even up here. As I explained earlier, the winter activities we want to offer won't be interrupted by inclement weather any more often than we experience in other seasons."

"I understand, Evelyn."

Oh, she hoped he did. More importantly, she needed him to trust her lifelong expertise in the area and her innovative expansion plans. Tate Cordell had surprised her when he'd reached out, but to date his continued interest in Cottonwood remained the most promising solution to propel the family business into profitable and sustainable territory for the long term.

There was a rapid tapping noise on his end before he spoke again. "I'll keep an eye on the weather and be in touch."

The call ended before she could say thank you.

Chilled again, she shoved her cell phone into her purse and put her glove back on for the dash across the parking lot.

Stan, a friendly face from high school, was the security guard on duty at the employee entrance. He held the door open for her as she rushed toward the building. "Evening," he said. "I hope you did all your storm prep before coming in."

She smothered the scream building in her throat. "Sure did," she replied. It wasn't Stan's fault that no one knew how to have a conversation about anything other than snowstorms right now. "Dad is all prepped at home and I have an overnight bag packed in the car, just in case I need to stay on and cover shifts."

"You really are set," he said with a smile. "Have a good shift, Evelyn."

She returned the sentiment as she walked away. Back here behind the scenes, the casino had designed a pleasant-enough area, though the focus was on utility rather than creating the posh experience everyone maintained out front for guests.

Stowing her coat and scarf in a locker, along with her boots, she slipped into the heels that completed the uniform and prepared for her shift. There weren't any new notices regarding players or problems, so when it was time, she strolled out to the casino.

It was her habit to take a circuit of the casino floor before taking her place at a table in the poker room. The routine helped her get a feel for the general vibe in and around the casino. Sometimes social events, big parties, or business groups amped up the energy and made everyone feel lucky. She had a similar habit when she guided tours with Cottonwood Adventures, always spending a few minutes by herself taking in the weather before loading gear or heading out.

Tonight, the guests seemed upbeat overall. She didn't hear any chatter about the weather, not even around the slot machines. There were the usual grumbles about luck, but the staff worked together to make sure no one turned mean or disruptive. Although the casino wasn't at full capacity, business was brisk, which was a good sign for her potential tips.

Evelyn opened her table for Texas Hold'em and the poker room host filled it immediately with four men she guessed were traveling together for business judging by the button-down shirts open at the collar and the khaki slacks that had probably been freshly creased this morning. The loafers were the big clue. No local in his right mind wore loafers in Deadwood at this time of year.

She found the group amusing with their friendly banter and superb poker-table manners. The various strategies they each attempted to convince the others to fold were hysterical. They played for an hour straight before one man excused himself to take a phone call from his wife.

Between hands, they discussed local attractions and dinner options. She dutifully recommended a casino restaurant without bringing up the adverse weather conditions. It would've been nice to suggest a winter walk or a sledding adventure, but Cottonwood didn't have those options yet. Not for the public anyway.

Other players came and went as seats opened up. The current game was tight as a drum and conversation declined as the betting increased. The intensity was palpable, though it was Evelyn's job to keep up the impression that every player in the game had an equal chance.

She relaxed a bit more as the hours ticked by and the players changed. Sure, she preferred working outside in tennis shoes or hiking boots instead of heels, but on days like today, the casino had become her salvation.

In here, with no clocks, she could pretend she wasn't running out of time for the business or for her personal goals. Her only task was to perpetuate the illusion that a life-changing jackpot was almost within reach. Beyond the tips, a shift at the casino also gave her a marvelous break from the constant news and weather warnings for the area. A customer might mention it in passing, but then someone would change the bet, or grimace, and the focus would shift back to the game.

There could be one snowflake or three feet of snow or even snowmageddon blowing outside. None of that mattered in the casino. People around town might complain about 'casino morals' but she'd learned that, for her, it was a slice of bliss. She dealt the cards, players won and lost, she dealt more cards, and the tips added up.

Did she want this forever? Not a chance. But right now, dealing at the Silver Aces was her best option. Maintenance expenses, equipment upkeep and property taxes didn't go into hibernation after the last leaf walk in the fall.

"Call," one of the men at her table declared with unmistakable excitement and only three cards turned up. There was a rumble of disappointment around the table followed by relatively sincere congratulations as the winner showed his hand.

Evelyn suppressed a smile as the winner gathered his chips. He took his time stacking the chips into his tray and then finally slid out of his seat, tossing a mock salute to the losing players.

Groans and complaints erupted from the remaining players. Everyone wanted a chance to change their luck.

"Know when to quit, that's my motto," the winner said. "There's a song about that right?"

"More than one," she replied.

With a wink, he slid a hundred-dollar chip her way as a tip.

"Thank you. It was a pleasure having you at the Silver Aces." Evelyn delivered the standard response politely when inside she was doing a dance of joy.

When the remaining players were settled again, she pulled the freshly shuffled deck from the automatic shuffler and prepared to deal the next game. She didn't need a clock to know her break was due after this game, her aching feet and back kept time for her. Tonight, she was looking forward to getting to the break room so she could check her phone. She wanted to make sure her dad was all right and, with luck, there would be an email from Tate with new post-storm options for tour times.

"Pardon me. Is it too late to slide in for this hand?"

She shot a quick glance at the poker room host and confirmed the customer was in the right place. Giving the man a nod to take the seat, she waited for him to post his minimum bet and then she dealt him in.

"Evelyn Cotton," he said as the players checked their cards. "Wow. It's really you."

That voice filtered through her senses, a sweet memory and brand new at the same time. Her head snapped up and she was immediately caught in a bright, laser-blue gaze. Those familiar eyes seemed to freeze time, stopping it short and pitching her backward.

Wyatt Jameson.

This was the last place on earth she'd expect to see him. Of course she'd given up on ever seeing him again, period. What had she done so wrong that fate or luck or whatever dumped him at her table? Her gaze swept over the room. Surely there had been another dealer with an open seat.

Somehow, she forced her attention back to the game. Verifying bets on the first round were complete, she turned up three cards in the middle of the table. For the first time since she'd gone solo as a dealer in this room her stomach churned with something just shy of panic.

"How have you been?" he asked after placing his second-round bet.

"Fabulous." The audacity of the man to walk in here and act as if they were old friends who'd simply lost touch.

She dealt the turn, adding the fourth card to the middle of the table. Reading her players, she gave a nod acknowledging one player raising the bet and another player folding. Wyatt added chips, staying in the game.

With an effort, she wrenched her gaze from his. She hadn't seen those stunning eyes since the night they'd graduated high school. Eleven long, lonely years without a word from the guy who'd been her best friend *and* her boyfriend. During those last two years of high school, she'd given him her heart and her virginity, shared all of her dreams and the worst of her fears. She'd bared her soul to him, revealing all of that and her budding expectations for the two of them.

Dealing the river, she turned up the fifth card in the middle of the table and called for final bets.

As each player made a bet or folded, she called for the showdown, less surprised than she should've been when

Wyatt won. While her mind whirled over what brought Wyatt back to Deadwood, she cleared the table of cards and chips and reset for the next game.

Growing up had not been easy for him. As his best friend, she'd caught glimpses of the rocky home life he'd endured on a daily basis. Still, in her heart there had been an understanding between them, and she'd been crushed when he'd walked away, with zero explanation.

Eleven years of silence. No letters or calls. He'd simply excised himself from both Deadwood and her in one shocking move. She'd been shattered more than heartbroken. He'd been the one person she'd counted on and confided in and she'd thought...

Well, clearly what she'd thought had been irrelevant.

By some miracle her hands didn't falter in the next deal. Muscle memory was a wonderful thing, she supposed. She should've been focused on the game and the other players, yet one question screeched incessantly through her mind: why was he here?

"What brings you to the Silver Aces this evening, Mr. Jameson," she said, oozing professional courtesy. If they'd met on the street she might have tackled him. She indulged in a quick fantasy of wrapping her hands around his throat until that sexy half-grin disappeared.

"Mr. Jameson? That's my dad's name. You always called me Wyatt." He smiled at the other players. "We went to high school together."

That earned both of them a round of vaguely curious murmurs and glances from the others at the table. Evelyn called for opening bets, motioning to him as she would any other overly-chatty player and moving the game along. The casino only made money when the cards and money were flowing, and the casino was her priority, not unanswerable questions.

This time Wyatt lost. She mentally gave Lady Luck a high five. Normally winning or losing only troubled her if a player was rude or belligerent about it. Not this time. As soon as she reached the relative privacy of the breakroom, she was going to give in to the whoop of delight swirling inside her.

Her thoughts might be mildly inappropriate, but no one would know or care. Especially not Wyatt. If he'd cared about her at all, he would've taken a minute to say goodbye before walking out of her life.

Her replacement walked up, timing the changeover perfectly. "That's it for me, gentleman." She smiled at each of the men around her table, including Wyatt, as she gathered her tips, including the chip from Wyatt. "It's been a pleasure and I wish each of you the best of luck here at the Silver Aces."

Doing the job well was far more important, and more mature, than indulging her childish vindictive streak and sticking out her tongue as she walked by her old flame.

Her father hated that she spent the off-season in the casino but without the seasonal work, they would've lost the business five years ago. She'd long ago stopped pointing out that her expansion ideas would put an end to her days of dealing poker. That line of thinking only created more resentment, one thing her personal life didn't need more of, so she cut it short.

There was a petty victory cheer and a dance of joy in her immediate future just as soon as she exited the casino floor.

"Evie?"

She flinched at the sound of the nickname that was used so rarely these days. Of course Wyatt had followed her. Of course he would revert to that old familiarity, sweeping her back to the days when they'd thought they were unstoppable and love would last forever. She walked on, refusing to turn around.

"Can we talk?"

"No." *No, no, no!* The hurt and angry teenager standing guard at the wall she'd build around her heart screamed. He didn't deserve another minute of her time.

"Please?" He fell into step beside her.

Slot machines chimed and jingled all around them. Lights flashed and a ticker high on the wall showed the odds on the upcoming heavyweight boxing match in Las Vegas as well as a tennis tournament in Shanghai.

All of that overwhelming stimulus and yet her senses were dialed in on Wyatt. The natural feel of him striding beside her and the enticing scent of his skin drew her back. Why? After eleven years, neither of those factors should be familiar. They were both different people, two adults on paths that should never intersect.

As the past threatened to swamp her, she considered what *had* changed. His youthful athletic build had filled out. That short beard sculpting his jaw made her fingers tingle with the urge to touch. There was a subtle hitch in his gait that she couldn't quite pin down. He was in a casino, for crying out loud, and playing poker with the skill of a man who did so regularly.

That stopped her. She gathered her composure and schooled her expression as she faced him. She was still on the floor, and therefore still required to maintain an upbeat, positive experience for every guest. Her feelings were irrelevant. The security cameras catching this exchange from every possible angle would only see a valued customer speaking with an employee. Wyatt hadn't taken a threatening position or been rude. She had to respond properly.

"Of course we can talk." She smiled. Cool, detached. "What would you like to discuss, Mr. Jameson?"

Flags of color stained his bold cheekbones and his lips flat-lined, framed by the fashionably scruffy beard.

"Evie—"

"Ms. Cotton," she corrected. "Please. We pride ourselves on our superb and always-appropriate customer service, Mr. Jameson."

"Would you stop?" He crowded her without moving a muscle. "It's me."

Yes, that was exactly why this entire encounter pushed the needle well beyond bizarre. "Are you with the weather service now or something?" It was the only plausible explanation she could think of for Wyatt's appearance in a Deadwood casino.

"What?" He shook his head. "No. There has to be somewhere we can speak privately." His voice rumbled over her, abrading her senses as effectively as his whiskers might. If she gave him the chance to get that close. Which she couldn't do here. Or anywhere.

While holding the professional smile, she shook her head slightly. "Not here."

For her 'here' included the casino, the shops, the restaurants and Deadwood as a whole. She wouldn't go anywhere with him. Couldn't. Being this close, recognizing the flare of heat in his blue gaze, made her want to forget everything he'd put her through and hit a reset switch.

She knew better, had to cling to logic and reason, even if her body was a traitor and didn't care about the way he'd crushed her heart. Yes, he looked good enough to eat and the slight hitch in his step somehow added to the swagger.

"Maybe a manager can be of more assistance," she suggested.

"Damn it, Evie. We were friends."

"We were." She folded her hands at her waist to keep them still while she waited for whatever he had to say.

"I'd like to reconnect." His gaze turned intense and she had the feeling she was supposed to parse out some meaning in what he *wasn't* saying. "At least let me buy you a coffee?"

"No, thank you."

His nostrils flared and his gaze narrowed. "I deserve that."

And more. She smiled when she wanted to snarl. "You deserve the best experience possible at the—"

"Please don't say it." He tucked his hands into his pockets, that blue gaze slicing right through her. "You're at work, I respect that." He glanced over her head, scanning the rows of slot machines.

Old habits, she supposed. At least now he was old enough to be in here legally to look around. His mom had been gone at least three years now. There had been an obituary in the paper and a graveside service. Evelyn hadn't attended the service, but she'd sent a sympathy card and a donation from Cottonwood Adventures.

"When are you off?"

"I'm afraid it's all hands on deck through the storm," she said. It might be true, but she wouldn't know for sure until she actually got to the breakroom. As much as she didn't want to deal with six feet or more of snow, she could use the extra shifts.

"You expect me to believe you're working straight through for the next three days."

"That's right." She dared him to contradict her. "Minimum."

"I see." He rocked back on his heels. "Sounds like an abuse of the work force. Maybe I should call it in."

"Is that what you do now? Go around causing trouble for happy casino employees?"

"You're not happy here," he stated with too much confidence.

Her chin lifted. She wasn't *unhappy* here and she didn't owe him any explanations about why dealing poker was an important part of her life. "My happiness isn't your concern anymore." She pushed the words through her clenched teeth and tight smile.

He reeled as if she'd slapped him. If only. Maybe she should agree to meet him somewhere. It would have to be somewhere outside and well off the established trails where she could finally let loose with all the pain-filled words and hateful thoughts she'd aimed his way through the years.

That bubble of old hurt and anger swelled in her chest and it took every ounce of willpower to keep her temper locked down while they were in public. At last, the bubble popped, leaving her weary with herself and with him. She was over Wyatt. It had been eleven years. What kind of loser would still be so desperately hung up on a high school boyfriend?

"If you'll excuse me."

"Come with me." Again his gaze swept the area behind her.

"No, thank you." If she didn't know better, she'd think he was part of the casino security team. Whatever he was looking for was none of her business. They weren't a couple anymore. "I really need to take what's left of my break."

His eyes locked with hers. "Evie, please."

A piece of her heart lurched toward him, hammering against the walls she'd built to protect herself. "I can't," she repeated, managing not to rub the pain in her breastbone. "If you're only here because of me, you need to go."

She turned on her heel and strode toward the employees-only door. As if he didn't matter at all.

Once she was through and out of his reach, she leaned against the cool wall. She'd expected walking away from him to feel better. Instead, she wanted to curl up in a corner and cry. Or run back into his arms. Would his embrace be familiar or different? She couldn't deny he'd changed.

Grown. Matured. All those things she'd thought she'd done too.

The door swung open as one of her coworkers walked through and she peeked out, startled to see Wyatt still standing there. Almost as if he was keeping watch or waiting for her.

Absurd. He'd leave. He'd go back to the tables. When it came to leaving her behind, Wyatt was a pro.

CHAPTER TWO

WYATT WAITED by the door after Evie slipped away from him. His fingers twitched, recalling the silk of her long auburn hair. She'd worn it down tonight, the glossy waves brushing her shoulders. The sight tempted him. He couldn't leave her alone, though she clearly wanted him out of the casino and her life, relegated to some dusty old box in the corner of her mind where she never had to look at him again.

He couldn't blame her. Being gone for eleven years, he hadn't expected to run into anyone who would recognize him, especially not in a casino. Based on the timing of this job, he thought he might get in and out of Deadwood without bumping into Evie at all.

No such luck.

What really stung was discovering the soul-deep attraction and affection that had burned so brightly when they were teenagers was all one-sided now. When she spoke to him, she might as well be talking to any other gambler. Her beautiful gray eyes, once so familiar, hadn't so much as flickered with the old warmth or passion she'd once shared so openly with him.

He folded his arms over his chest, thinking about how he might crack through her veneer of professional interest and flat smile. Where was his Evie? The woman still haunted his memories and dreams all these years later. At eighteen he'd left everything in Deadwood behind only to discover she was as essential as oxygen to him.

He never should have agreed to come back.

If he could rewind and do things differently, he never would've hurt her. He'd had to leave Deadwood, but he could've done it with more care for her. She'd been his only salvation in those unbearable last few months of high school. The two of them had been inseparable, spending hours with homework or working, constantly brainstorming fresh ideas for her family business, what they would change, when and how it would grow into a regional destination.

As far as he could tell during the prep for this trip, Cottonwood Adventures offered pretty much the same tours and events they'd offered when he'd left. He knew it had nothing to do with him, but he couldn't help wondering why Evie bailed on her ideas for growth.

At this rate, he'd never know. Contrary to her assessment, he'd never stopped caring for her or her happiness. Maybe he didn't have the right to demonstrate that concern, but he wouldn't let her aggravation with his choices interfere with his purpose tonight.

He couldn't leave. Not until she made it home safely tonight and promised to stay away from the casino for the next few days.

Better if he could convince her to quit and never come back. She shouldn't be here at all. Well, maybe as a customer, but never as an employee. When he spotted her dealing poker on his second walk-through of the casino for his current assignment, his stomach had cramped so hard he'd nearly doubled over. Had she forgotten what happened when gambling and the pursuit of a jackpot got the best of someone?

Knowing what was coming, the trouble that had nothing to do with the winter storm, he hadn't seen another option except to sit down and play at her table. Unfortunately, her relief arrived before he'd found the right way to warn her off.

In his pocket, his phone buzzed again and he glanced toward the slot machines, looking for the FBI agent posing as a casino guest while watching his back. Agent Noelle Pickering, second in command on her team of four, had been the first to reach out to him about this assignment. She wore an emerald sweater and black slacks, her short blond hair gleaming under the lights. At the moment, her phone was at her ear.

"What are you up to?" she asked. "We aren't covering your poker losses."

"Didn't ask you to," he said. Besides he was modestly ahead at the moment. "Saw an old friend," he said. It wasn't like his ties to Evie were a secret.

"You might want to delay the old flame hookup routine until this is over," Pickering said.

"Right." He should've expected the FBI had done as much homework on him as they had on their target.

"We picked up another call on the phone tap. Evelyn Cotton might be part of the Cordell crew." He barely suppressed the automatic rejection of the absurd suggestion. If Cordell had contacted Evie it wasn't because she was interested in helping him steal a fortune in diamonds.

"Not their first communication," Pickering continued, as if she could read minds now. "And here she is, a casino employee. Sounds like she's into him."

Bull. That was just mean, even if Pickering was simply relaying facts.

Tate Cordell was a slick operator, that's all. He was using

Evie somehow. Anyone could change in eleven years—Wyatt was proof—but Evie would never willingly help a criminal. Cordell must be lining her up for backup or a distraction.

"Did they talk about the casino?"

"Not directly."

Wyatt nearly growled. "What did they discuss?"

"Money," Pickering said. "Watch yourself. We're counting on you."

He ended the call and tucked his phone away. Now he *had* to get Evie to open up before she found herself in the middle of an FBI investigation.

Like him.

This should've been a straightforward job. Infiltrate the Cordell crew, wait for them to rob the casino, and then lead them into FBI custody. In exchange for helping the FBI, Wyatt would get a percentage of the value of the diamonds recovered, money he needed to establish his fledgling private investigations firm.

He paced away from the door, in case Evie had access to the security camera. This new development between her and Cordell was seriously bad luck on a day when he needed things to roll his way. He gave himself a mental shake. Luck was the casino's stock in trade and rigged to favor the house. Wyatt couldn't rely on luck, good or bad. Stuff happened and a smart man dealt with it. Wyatt believed in thorough planning and intelligent execution of those plans.

He could credit bumping into Evelyn Cotton in this particular casino during his only return to Deadwood as the universe's idea of a grand joke. The universe wasn't all that funny.

He walked away from the slots, away from the gaming rooms and found a plush seating area near the retail area. Sinking into a deep couch, he pulled out his phone and did another search on Cottonwood Adventures, the company

Evie's family had owned and operated for generations. What had he missed the first time through?

That's where she should've been, outside running free and wild through the Black Hills. Whenever he thought of her, it was out on the creek or guiding a group on a walk through the trees, the colorful autumn leaves ablaze overhead. Winters had been for cleaning and repairing gear, for sledding and snowball fights.

What happened to drive her indoors to deal poker?

Today, the website showed an update that Cottonwood was closed for the season. Wyatt swore. Just two weeks ago, prepping for this trip, the site had advertised winter nature hikes. Evie didn't deal poker like a newbie and she hadn't been the least bit interested in cards or anything else when they were kids.

A text message reminder slid across his phone screen. Cordell was expecting the report of the casino and retail layout with initial observations on the staff. Within Cordell's crew, Wyatt was supposedly the first man in at the Silver Aces. He didn't actually believe the others weren't here, not with such a big storm closing in, but he played along.

"Fine," he muttered.

Maybe this thing with Evie didn't have to be a big deal. He knew that whatever Cordell was up to, she wasn't involved. So Wyatt had come face to face with the only person in this town whose opinion still mattered to him. He didn't have time to let a chance meeting turn into something significant.

His feet felt heavy as he made his next circuit around the casino floor, again taking a visual inventory of the rows of slots and layout of gaming tables. The Silver Aces had a pretty good vibe for a place built to suck in every dollar in the vicinity. He wasn't a big fan of casinos, knew firsthand how gambling wrecked homes, shredded hope and laid waste to happiness—present and future.

He dutifully sat down at a slot machine, his jaw clenched tight as he put in the token and hit the button. Lights flashed and the machine made noises as if the wheels spinning were mechanical rather than electrical.

No jackpot. He repeated the process, hitting that big flashy button time and again. He added money and did his rudimentary part in a system designed to separate him from his cash. While he ignored the machine, his mind drifted back to Evie, the girl who'd been his best friend all through school.

Then more than friends.

Back then, Evie had shared his distaste and distrust for the casino industry. Sure it brought jobs and money into Deadwood, but no one would ever convince him that the potential for serious collateral damage to local families was worth it.

His cell phone hummed in his pocket as the timer he'd set went off. He yanked his head out of the past. Being surprised could be deadly on this assignment and for the investigations business as a whole. The job ahead of him and the potential reward was too important to botch because he wasn't focused.

Adding more tokens to the slot machine, he made mental notes of the patterns between waitresses, security, and staff moving money.

In the row behind him a slot machine went off with a big payout. Shouts of delighted shock and joy went up around the winner. Wyatt pretended to be as enthused and interested as the other patrons, though he stayed in his seat.

Like mother like son, he supposed. In fourth grade he'd broken his wrist on the playground during recess and Evie's mom had shown up at the hospital, kept him calm, and taken him home after the x-rays were complete and the cast was set. Evie's dad, along with one of his friends on the Deadwood police force, had finally pried Rosemary Jameson away from her favorite slot machine.

Working the plan Cordell outlined, Wyatt played until he was up a few hundred dollars and then left the slots. Passing the gaming rooms, he saw Evie was back at work. This time he stayed far away. From her, from the tables.

He moseyed along, toward the retail area where everything a person could imagine was emblazoned with the Silver Aces logo. He wasn't the souvenir type, hadn't been many places that he wanted to remember fondly. Not Deadwood. Not Afghanistan. Definitely not the military installations where he'd been stationed through his ten-year career.

He passed the jewelry store, Cordell's planned target, noting the number and positions of the armed guards. Only one man was in uniform. Two others wore dark suits and stern expressions. If their goal was blending in, they'd failed. Knowing the men in suits were the bigger threat and more likely trained to notice curious people, Wyatt didn't linger. He passed the display window and strolled on through the retail area that linked the casino with the hotel.

The silence and solitude in the elevator were welcome. He really had to find a way to be comfortable around people and crowds again. An easier task if he had any trust left to give. Odds were good he had a more cynical outlook on people than the suits downstairs guarding the jewelry store display.

In his room, he jotted a few notes while waiting to make his scheduled check-in call. He kicked off his shoes and rocked forward and back on his feet, stretching out the aching muscles and tendons. Although it was all compensatory pain and far less than he usually dealt with, it was still pain. If he let it get ahead of him, it impaired his quick-thinking and reaction time.

On this job, he couldn't risk either weakness.

The room phone on the nightstand rang once. He stared at it. Had to be a wrong number since all communication with both the FBI and Cordell was limited to the two cell phones he carried.

Maybe it was Evie a small voice in his head suggested. And maybe he was a complete fool.

Still, her face filled his mind along with memories of her soft, summer kisses under dappled sunlight near the creek that ran behind her house. Did she think of him when she walked that way? Or had she replaced those memories with new ones?

He was suddenly and inexplicably jealous of some faceless man kissing Evie's petal-soft lips.

At the sound of a cell phone, he pulled himself back to the task at hand and picked up the burner phone. "You've got Jameson," he answered.

"You know what to do," the voice on the other end of the line said. One of Cordell's assistants always answered these calls. If Cordell thought that would somehow distance him from any criminal charges, he was woefully misinformed.

"Target is in place," Wyatt reported. A portion of the diamonds the crew meant to steal were prominently on display in the window. Admirers were urged to come into the store and see the famed Mae West Solitaire, an incredible stone, valued in the neighborhood of one million dollars thanks to her reputation along with the diamond's weight and setting. "You'll have the full twenty-four hour cycle report for the floor by morning. So far one uniform and two plain clothes at all times."

"Candy from a baby," Cordell's voice drifted from the background.

Wyatt bit back a scathing retort. Not his job to make them successful thieves. Well, not really. His primary job was to guide them out of the area. "Looks that way," he managed, hoping it sounded convincing.

After this job, he could pick and choose where to live. How to live. Thanks to the internet, he'd been able to start his investigations business with nothing more than his laptop and a cell phone.

"What about the weather?" Cordell asked, his voice booming through the phone.

Wyatt pulled the phone from his ear and scowled. Cordell had picked up the device on his end and he sounded concerned. "What about it?" The reports were being broadcast nationwide, updates broadcast hourly everywhere except the casino floor. If they were already in town as Wyatt assumed, they should have heard the latest local warnings.

"You grew up around there," Cordell snapped. "Do we have a problem?"

Was the man actually unable to comprehend the dire snowfall warnings? "The better question is what can we change to cope with it," Wyatt hedged. "Do you want to put this off for a few days?" The diamonds were scheduled to be here for another week.

"No. A delay is not an option."

Wyatt had assumed from the start Cordell had a buyer lined up. A buyer who wouldn't tolerate any excuse, not even a massive winter storm. The information might give Pickering a fresh angle to work.

"Well, there is a risk that the main roadway will be closed," he allowed, unsure what Cordell wanted to hear.

Anyone who bothered to take a drive through the Black Hills would notice paved roadways weren't prevalent. If the main highway was blocked Wyatt would have to find another way to the rendezvous point Cordell had specified a few miles north of Deadwood. With the storm bearing down on the area, that could get tricky.

"If you want your cut, you'll get us out."

"I'm aware," Wyatt said. "There are alternate routes. I was just taking a look," he lied. The next thing on his agenda tonight was locating the best way to send Cordell and his crew straight to jail. "If everyone is in place on time, I'll get us all out as promised."

"We know what we're doing." Cordell made a noise that rang a little too close to a villainous chuckle and sent a ripple of dread across the back of Wyatt's neck.

The call ended. Finally.

Wyatt scrubbed away the dread and dropped the phone on the hotel dresser. This was *not* his idea of a good time. If he'd ever thought working with the FBI might be entertaining, the pressing storm and Cordell's laugh cured that misconception.

He thought of Evie downstairs dealing poker and swore. He wondered what it would take to read the reports on the calls between her and Cordell. Dumb question. Pickering and her team might agree, but at what cost? He didn't want to be drawn into another case. No, he'd cash his check and move on with his life.

One of these days he would decide where to live that life. Not here. If he'd harbored any hope of coming home, Evie's reaction had crushed that. Clearly, she wasn't pleased to see him again. He doubted she'd hesitate to turn him in if she realized he was working with thieves.

In forty-eight hours, when it came out that he was tied to the diamond theft, she'd hate him more than ever. Why did that twist him up? He'd wrecked everything all by himself when he'd run away.

It shouldn't matter. He couldn't let her low opinion of him interfere with the work. Too much was riding on this entire operation. Turning on the television, he found the weather channel. He'd just flopped back on the bed to await the next update on Winter Storm Holly, when someone knocked at the door.

Of course. This would be Pickering or one of the other agents, eager to go over every word and inflection of his chat with Cordell. The man must have really embarrassed them on some previous occasion to have them so intent on capture.

He should probably do something fun during his stay in an upscale hotel on the government's dime. According to the schedule, he'd have tomorrow to himself, then the robbery the day after. Too bad Cottonwood didn't have tours available.

Resigned, he flung the door open without checking who was on the other side. He barely caught back the terse greeting when he saw it was Evie standing there instead of agent Pickering.

She jerked, her face going pale. "Sorry. This is a bad time," she said. "Bad idea," she mumbled, backing away into the hallway.

"Evie," he breathed. His heart seemed stuck in his chest. "I thought..." He shook his head. "Doesn't matter. I wasn't expecting you."

"I'm afraid to ask who you were expecting."

"Come, in. It's fine." It was a terrible time and a stupid idea after Pickering all but said Evie was involved with Cordell. "Do you want to come in?"

"Um. No, thanks." She didn't move away from the door. "I just, um... I made a mistake."

"Come inside, Evelyn. Please."

"I really can't. Not while I'm in uniform." She wrapped the open panels of her coat tightly around her, as if hiding as much of that uniform as possible. Her chin came up, but compassion glowed in those soft gray eyes. "I just wanted to say... to tell you that this—me working here—wasn't something I planned on. It became a necessity."

His heart settled back into place and the normal rhythm he generally ignored. "Evie, I'd never judge you."

She rolled her eyes. "We both know that's exactly what you did the moment you saw me downstairs."

He leaned against the door jamb. "Then it was mutual. You were appalled to see me playing poker."

"I might have been annoyed you won the first hand," she confessed.

His amusement, that sweet familiarity of talking with his best friend evaporated when Agent Pickering strolled down the hallway. She tossed him a warning look from behind Evie. Damn it. He was in for a ton of questions about his motives and intentions if he couldn't provide the answers she was after about Cordell and Evie.

"Why?"

She tugged the zipper on her coat up and down a few inches. "Probably because I'm petty," she confessed.

"No." He fought a smile. "Why did working here become necessity?"

"Oh." Her straight white teeth pinched her lower lip. "Long story short, we need the money. For the business and taxes and stuff."

"What about all your expansion plans? Just a couple weeks ago you had sledding tours listed."

"You looked me up?"

He smiled now. "I couldn't come back to Deadwood and not look you up. I wanted to see you." Although seeing her had been the exact opposite of his actual intent on this trip, he would always *want* to see Evie.

"It was BYOS."

"Bring Your Own Sled?" She nodded. "So?"

She sighed and did the thing with the zipper again. "That's my problem, Wyatt. I just wanted to tell you about this." She leaned close and lowered her voice. "It's only winters. If I had another option, I wouldn't be here. But I don't want to lose the business."

"That bad?"

Her gaze dropped to the patterned carpet between them and she shrugged. "It's only winters," she repeated.

Before he could overthink it, he caught her hand and placed it on the open door. "Hold this." Swiveling around and darting into the room, he grabbed his coat. "Your shift is over?"

She nodded.

"The snow's been getting heavier," he reminded her. "Are the roads clear enough to get home?"

Another bob of her chin.

"I'll walk you to your car."

"For old time's sake?" She cocked her head, skeptical.

The doubt in her gaze hollowed him out and regrets flooded into the void. When they'd been together, she'd trusted him completely. And he'd thrown away that precious gift with a shameful carelessness. And now she was here trying to explain her actions, decisions he guessed she'd been forced to make. He didn't deserve her. And she didn't deserve to be used by him, Cordell, the FBI or anyone else.

"Something like that." He didn't touch her as they walked to the elevator. It felt wrong, as if a joint was out of place. Present, but not functioning properly. In the past they held hands at every opportunity. "Are you even sure you can make it home tonight?"

"And back again in the morning," she quipped. "Tomorrow night could be a different story."

They stepped into the car when it arrived, suspending conversation with other guests around.

"I appreciate your concern," she said as they walked toward the retail section of the resort.

"But I lost the right to have an opinion about your life

and choices," he finished for her. "A situation I regret," he added. "Since we seem to be sharing." The lighting had been dialed down, but all of the stores they passed were open. "Does anything in this place ever close?"

"Of course." She pointed to a subtle sign near the door of the next store. "The hours are posted, though it strikes me as hypocritical since there isn't a single clock anywhere in the guest areas."

"I guess everyone has a phone or smart watch." And he just realized he'd left both of his devices upstairs in the room.

"True." She turned down a short hallway toward an exit sign and he followed. "The employee lot is this way."

It was a part of the casino he hadn't explored. Cordell demanded reports on security, not general employee habits. Wyatt figured the FBI had eyes on every casino entrance, so he kept his focus limited to his role.

On the other side of the doors, the world was coated with white. "Maybe you should stay over," he said. "It's already piling up."

"You sound like a tourist," she joked.

"I feel like one after all this time."

"Well then I recommend a winter walk led by Cottonwood Adventures to get familiar with the area again. Once the storm passes."

He'd love to spend more time with Evie if she'd allow it. "Seriously?"

"I wish." There was a razor-sharp edge on each word. "Believe me, I'd rather be guiding tours."

"Even in this weather?" he asked.

"Yes." She paused a few paces from the automatic door and the guard standing by. Zipping up her coat, she adjusted her scarf and pulled on gloves. "You're familiar with snowmania. This storm can't possibly be as bad as they're saying," she grumbled. "It'll blow itself out before it gets to us."

He hoped she was right, if only so he could be done with Cordell and his crew. "You'll take precautions though?" he asked, buttoning his coat.

"I'm not an idiot." She tugged her hood up over her hair. "Are you staying or getting out ahead of it?"

He couldn't tell her he was planning to be part of a different problem for the casino.

"I'll be here a few days." He tugged his gloves over his hands.

Her eyebrows arched. "Why?"

"Business." It wasn't a lie, though even the truth left a bitter taste on his tongue. "Let's go."

A burst of cold air lashed them as the doors parted and, experts at bad weather, they leaned into it. Most women would fuss or squeal. Despite the scarf, he knew Evie's lips curved into a smile. Her eyes sparkled and her cheeks rose a fraction. She was meant for the outdoors. When they were much younger, he'd had fanciful thoughts about her being some sort of woodland fairy. He'd never been dumb enough to voice the bizarre thought, but it hit him again right now.

This was Evie at her best and in her element, regardless of weather conditions. She had a faultless sense of direction and unparalleled courage. They used to joke you could send her up a creek without a paddle and she'd smile the whole way.

Naturally, her car was parked at the end of a row, well away from the building. She pressed the button on the key fob and the lights flashed as the doors unlocked. Neither of them moved.

"You didn't have to walk me all the way out."

"Of course I did." The air had enough bite to make it uncomfortable to talk and he needed to convince her to go home and stay there. "You'll need some help clearing the windows." He owed her more than a few kind gestures. He owed her explanations.

She seemed to sense it. Maybe eleven years didn't amount to a permanent divide after all. "Get in and talk while the car warms up."

He didn't need an engraved invitation. Hustling around the car, he slid into the passenger seat. She drove a crossover that hadn't been new in some time. He imagined it handled the terrain and demands of the outdoor business well.

She started the engine and turned on the defrosters for the front and rear. The fan labored and whined and he wondered if it was up to the task. When she picked up a snow brush from behind her seat, he took it from her. "Let me."

"It's not just winters," she blurted.

He pulled the door closed, watching her.

She tugged the scarf away from her face. "We're about one season away from losing everything. Dealing poker is the only way to keep us going until spring. I've worked up some private tours and ala carte contracts, but the salary and tips are the bread and butter right now."

His stomach dropped at her mention of private tours. Did the FBI misinterpret Cordell and Evie working out fees for a private tour? It made sense. Evie wasn't a thief, no matter how dire things were with Cottonwood. If that was the case, Cordell wasn't looking for a snowy landscape for the perfect picture. More likely that snake was hoping to prevent Wyatt's double-cross.

"Ala carte? What about your plans for year-round events?"

She let her head fall back against the seat. "A kid's plan," she said.

"That's your father talking." Wyatt remembered brainstorming with Evie about all sorts of improvements and innovations that would appeal to the next generation of adventuring customers.

"You're not wrong," she said. "Neither is he. Winter

excursions require winter gear and equipment. Dale Cotton doesn't subscribe to the 'takes money to make money' theory. We both had to step up. He restores furniture and I found a job that pays."

Wyatt hated that Evie was sacrificing herself. "Wow." Eleven years ago her working in any capacity at the casinos would've broken their friendship. He was a different man now.

"I'm sorry," she said, her gaze on the snow blowing across the glow of light from the parking lamp overhead.

"Don't be. You have good plans for Cottonwood Adventures. If this is what it takes, consider it a phase." But why did the universe have to plant her here, in the casino targeted for a big robbery. A robbery he was knotted up in.

"You must hate me."

"Please." He snorted. "The opposite seems more likely." Her reaction to him earlier was plenty of proof. "You were fuming from the moment you recognized me."

She punched his shoulder. Hard. Confirming his assessment. "You left without a word. Not one letter or phone call." She rubbed her reddening nose. "I had to hear everything from the paper."

It would've been easier if she'd shouted at him. The aching emotion in her quiet voice was too much. "I had to leave." Unlike her, he didn't have a good explanation for his choices. At the time, he'd thought not saying goodbye to his best friend was the only way to go through with it. Staying wasn't an option and leaving wasn't all that he'd hoped for.

"What did you hear in the paper?" He regretted the question immediately. He wasn't fishing for compliments, he was supposed to be getting her out of harm's way without tipping her off.

"Local boy joins the Army and becomes a hero, that kind of thing," she replied.

"I'm surprised they bothered." Uneasy, he adjusted the vent shooting hot air at him. "My branch of the Jameson family tree wasn't exactly popular." His mother had gambled the family into such a deep hole they'd lost the house and everything that had once been good inside it.

Evie had been his lifeline, his last tether to a better reality. Evie's father had talked to him about enlisting, about creating a fresh start and building a foundation his mother couldn't touch.

It was go... or be consumed by her weakness. There were nights—plenty of them that first year—when he wondered if Dale had ever told Evie about those talks, about the advice that pushed Wyatt out of Deadwood toward a better life. Probably not. Dale would've expected Wyatt to explain and he'd never found the words.

Evie's place was here. For a time, Wyatt had been convinced his place was here, by her side, helping her take Cottonwood Adventures to the next level.

"You were my best friend, Wyatt." Her voice was barely audible over the blowing fans and he wondered if she meant for him to hear the words at all. "My heart broke over you. I... I don't think I can go have coffee or a drink because deep down a part of me wants to forget the last eleven years of silence." She sucked in a breath and bit her lip. On the exhale she faced him. "For as long as you're in town, can we just pretend we *don't* know each other?"

"Evie—" It would be safer for her and yet, he resisted. He couldn't just ignore what might be his only chance to make up for his mistakes.

"I mean it," she said. "Eleven years is a lot of time and distance. We're different people now, really. You've been all over the world and I've been right here. Call me a coward, but I'll only get hurt if I try to reconnect with you right now."

She was no coward. Just the opposite. "I should tell you—"

She cut him off. "Don't tell me anything. Just be yourself, be the town hero. Do whatever you're here to do, just do it well away from me."

If he'd been surprised to see her dealing poker, he was absolutely shocked now. What she proposed was for the best on several levels. With the storm coming in, and the robbery in the offing, staying away from her simplified everything. This way Cordell couldn't drag her into his plans. "You're sure that's what you want?"

"It is."

How could he argue with her? She deserved to dictate terms now when he'd never given her a shot before. "You'll go home and ride out the storm there?"

"That's the plan," she replied.

A plan that kept her away from the casino without him blowing his cover by telling her the whole sordid tale. Agent Pickering could get herself out to the Cotton place if she wanted clarity about Evie and Cordell.

"Promise me you'll stay home through the storm?"

She ran her gloved hands over the steering wheel, not meeting his gaze. "I promise."

He gripped the door handle. "I loved you, Evie. We were only kids, but still. I know I hurt you, the way I left, but I've never wanted anything less than the best for you. I swear it."

CHAPTER THREE

EVIE WAS grateful for the quick flash of cold air as Wyatt got out of her car. It cooled her cheeks and eased the sting of tears in her eyes. "I loved you too," she whispered to the empty car.

She'd thought she was all cried out when it came to Wyatt Jameson, but she found a supply of tears ready to spill over at the next opportunity. Which was not here while the man was clearing her windows. Driving home in the snow would be bad enough without tear-blurred vision and sadness.

On a deep breath, she swiped the moisture from her cheeks. She was proud of herself for clearly stating her reasons for avoiding any kind of a reunion. For not letting the bitterness spill out and ruin a friendly moment. But she didn't want a gold star for maturity. She wanted the impossible, she wanted her friend back. That seemed to be her natural default, wanting things she didn't have any control over.

Wyatt finished dusting the snow off her windows and returned the brush. "Drive safe."

"I will. Take care," she managed.

And then it was over. She put the car in gear and left the

parking lot. Spending any more time with Wyatt would be the worst. She had a business to save. Investors to woo and team-building contracts to finalize. Wyatt was in the past and there were too many broken promises between them to recover. She would not look back, would not watch him trudge back to the casino.

Overhead the night sky was loaded with heavy clouds, an ever-present threat of the lousy weather to come. Lights from the streets, stores, and hotels along the main road created a sparkling kaleidoscope on the fresh snow. The road crews would be working around the clock plowing and salting the roads if the storm stayed on track.

Stopped at a traffic light, she forced herself to look back at her time with Wyatt objectively. They'd been teenagers, barely old enough to think through the haze of hormones and wild dreams. If he'd stayed here in town, there was no guarantee they could've made a relationship work. Between the struggles with his mother's gambling addiction and her dad's refusal of every new idea, maybe they would have crumbled.

Or stagnated.

An ending was an ending. Maybe it had been cleaner his way. The brief conversation had given her closure, which made her feel better. She'd looked him in the eyes and survived. And now she wouldn't see him again during his stay. They could both move on happy and guilt-free to bigger and better things.

The light changed to green and her tires spun in the slush despite the salt on the roads. Although it was late, she should probably get the chains on her tires when she got home. She rounded the bend and had to jerk the car to the shoulder to avoid an oncoming vehicle speeding by. Her tires slogged through the deeper accumulation of snow and icy slush on the side of the road and she skidded sideways through the lane while she tried to get back on course.

Holding her breath, Evie fought hard to keep the car on the right side of the road. Losing control here, on a blind curve, was a death wish in the making. She regained control and slowed down as much as she dared. Turning on her hazard flashers, she struggled through a few deep breaths as her heart rate returned to normal.

Her hands were sweating inside her gloves when she saw the first sign for Cottonwood Adventures. As she made the turn off the main highway, the back end fishtailed, but she got it under control, grateful to find the access road freshly plowed. Definitely time to get the chains back on the car.

Despite her bluster to the contrary, she was concerned about this storm. The bank accounts were so tight she needed every possible shift, every possible tip, and every possible private tour she could arrange.

She'd been so disappointed after her shift when a check of her email showed Tate hadn't rescheduled either an online meeting or an in-person tour. There wasn't any point in dwelling on it, but she was now kind of hoping Deadwood got smothered with snow and businesses closed altogether for a few days. That way the bank couldn't turn down her next loan application for the Cottonwood Adventures expansion.

Before she'd wrestled the finances and publicity plans from her father, he'd drained the reserve account in his effort to prove her expansion ideas were pointless. He'd run ads that weren't profitable and refused to take her advice about building a social media presence seriously. She did what she could but, in season, she was busy from dawn to dusk as a guide. Not just because she was their best, but because it meant not paying someone else a salary and benefits.

The busyness of their spring, summer, and fall schedules also meant less time for networking with other tour companies in Deadwood. Some days, when she was overtired, it felt as if Dale wanted her to fail so he could close up shop and be done. If that happened, she'd be lost. More lost than when Wyatt had left town.

She had options. Another adventure company would put her to work and, Sarah, her manager at the casino would happily take her full time, but her heart and hopes and dreams were all invested in Cottonwood's success.

Big snowflakes splatted against her windshield. Almost home. Could be worse, she reminded herself as her wiper blades cleared a path. She could be trying to drive on ice or through the wind and white-out conditions the forecasters predicted would create ten-foot drifts in places.

She hadn't seen a storm quite so severe in her lifetime, but she'd heard the stories. In Deadwood, winter storms often grew as time passed, similar to the way a fisherman talked about a catch. Although in the modern era there was usually photographic evidence of the snow.

Her thoughts wandering, she missed the driveway and had to stop and put the car in reverse. When her headlights hit the low snowbank she swore. The plow had overlooked the driveway as well. Instead of pushing the gathered snow to one side or the other, the driver had ignored the driveway entirely. Not unusual, but a bad sign if Holly did in fact hit them head on.

She drove through the small berm, backed up, and drove through again, flattening as much snow as possible before heading up to the house. The house was dark when she pulled up, but the porch lights were on at the main house and at the cottage they'd originally built for her grandmother.

Evie had moved in after college. The cottage wasn't fancy or chic, though she'd done plenty of updating. The biggest plus was the privacy and independence she gained. Breathing space. Without that, her relationship with her dad would've taken a disastrous dive over the nearest cliff.

The flipside of her father's stubbornness was his

predictability. Tonight wasn't the night to resent his deeply ingrained routine of leaving the light on for her. In her own way her stubborn streak matched his. Neither of them would give an inch on anything. She'd have to prove to him the winter events were worth the investment in good gear and smart advertising.

And she had nothing to lose by implementing her plan on a small scale just as soon as the worst of this storm blew through. In a few hours, over breakfast, she could tell her dad that the hospitality manager had agreed to a sledding day as a team-building exercise.

It was a coup on both fronts and the few people who'd overheard the plan had been enthused. Evie would be paid her base salary, plus the going rate as a guide and for two straight shifts she wouldn't have to work indoors. Assuming the sledding day went well, she could add testimonials to her final proposal for the casino to add it as a morale-building option for other departments.

That was the kind of creativity it would take to save and expand the business her father's grandfather had started with fishing trips and hunting expeditions. Not that Dale would embrace it. She could already hear his arguments about hiring quality people, drafting the appropriate legal releases and all the rest of it. Tomorrow was soon enough for that fight, though she'd long since given up asking why he was determined to impede her success at the very point when she should be taking over the business.

There was tradition and there was flat-out nonsense.

Remembering she wanted to get the chains on her tires tonight, she drove around to the barn that served as the Cottonwood business office and primary storage area. Parking, she cut the engine, irritated with herself when the keys rattled in her hand. She was still on edge after that near miss on the curve.

Better to blame her shakes on that non-incident than her talk with Wyatt.

Her boots sank into the gathering snow as she trudged over and unlocked the overhead door, sliding it up. It felt like the snow was coming down harder and she wished she was wearing her silk-weight long underwear.

She flipped on the overhead light and crossed to the wall-rack where they stored the tire chains. Three out of four tires were done when she heard something moving through the snow behind her. Jerking around, blinking snowflakes from her eyelashes, she saw Dale lowering his shotgun.

"Dad!" She pressed a hand to her heart. "What are you doing?"

"The alarm system woke me up with that open-door message."

"I'm sorry. I should've thought of that." She could've temporarily reset that feature from the panel in the barn.

"No matter. I only came out because the first time it went off someone was fiddling with the back door."

"What?" She had the security system app on her phone and hadn't seen anything about a break-in attempt. "When?" Pushing to her feet, she hurried through the barn to the door that backed onto the woods surrounding their property.

"A few hours ago," he said trailing after her. "You were at the casino so I called Sheriff Russell. He came out and looked around, decided it must've been bored kids."

They must've been bored to come out this way to poke at a barn full of out of season camping gear, tools, and brochures. "Was anything taken?" She did a quick visual scan of the gear before checking that the door closed and locked properly. Nothing appeared to be out of place.

"Not that I could see." Dale tipped his head toward her car. "What are you doing with the chains?"

"Just making sure I can get to work tomorrow." She

turned off the bright overhead lights. She'd promised Wyatt she wouldn't go back, but it wasn't that simple. "I have a mid-day shift."

Dale muttered something most likely unflattering about the casino industry that she ignored. "You just got home." He turned toward the opening to watch the snow. "Coming down like this, chains won't be enough if the plows keep forgetting we live up this way."

"True." His obvious delight with that observation irked her. They needed her paychecks, whether or not he'd ever admit it. "That's why I'm headed back in. Tonight." She'd just decided. "The hotel has rooms for this kind of situation and I won't have to miss a shift."

Her dad stewed, his hands tight on the shotgun. For a split-second she worried for her car. "This is the off-season," he barked. "You can't go twenty-four-seven all year long and be healthy."

She gaped at him. This was a brand new argument and the novelty was almost refreshing. "The bills don't stop for the season, Dad."

"It was never a problem before." The words came out so hard he might as well be chewing gravel.

Before her mom died. "I know." Sympathy pulsed through Evelyn. Her dad was tough and spry, but at the core he was lonely without his wife. "Hop in and I'll give you a ride back to the house."

"I'm fine," he muttered. "Go on back up there if you have to. You're so sure you know what's best."

She ignored the jab, so tired of fighting over piddly stuff when they needed to hash out serious issues. "Get in the car, Dad." He wasn't even wearing gloves. "I'm not taking any chances with you."

She started the car for him and cranked the heater so he could be warm while she closed up the barn. With the security system reset, she climbed behind the wheel.

"I could've walked."

"I know. It's even uphill the whole way."

He snorted. "You're sassy tonight."

"Punchy after a long shift is more like it."

"Would we really be in that much financial trouble if you quit?" he asked.

So he did listen to her once in a while. She pulled to a stop at the front porch, put the car in Park, but she kept the engine running. "Yes. This time of year it's that close." She held up her hand, finger and thumb barely separated. "We have interested investors and a couple of experimental events that could turn into something lucrative, but—"

"We can't count money we don't have yet," he finished.

"That's right." She covered his hand, gave him a gentle squeeze. "You taught me that."

"Your mother did."

"Maybe take half the credit then," she teased. "I love you, Dad. I love this business. Our legacy. I can save it."

He pulled away, a frown puckering his bushy eyebrows. "You shouldn't have to. It's my job to provide, not yours."

Despite the late hour, she couldn't leave him while he was so gloomy. "You've been an excellent provider my whole life."

He tapped his boot against the floorboard, knocking off the snow. "Then we shouldn't be in financial duress."

Logically he was right. Equipment aged out, reservations cancelled, life happened. Her mom died and apparently so had his interest in living. The following season, her last year of college, he'd all but closed Cottonwood Adventures. It didn't help that they'd been divided on how to recover from those slumps.

She gripped the steering wheel, wishing she could shake some common sense into him. He could retire and let her handle things. "Let's go inside and talk."

"Y'know," he said, not moving. "I expected that Jameson boy to come back. Customers liked him. He could've sorted us out."

Any gentleness she'd felt toward her father evaporated. The car turned frigid, despite the heater blowing on high. "Wyatt was a good employee." It was the nicest, most neutral reply she could give. "And a good friend."

Wyatt had been her friend long before he'd become her boyfriend. Through the years, he'd earned her parents' trust and affection with his quick grin, wry sense of humor, and his willingness to help out. Dale and Tess generously opened their home and hearts and filled the role of warm, loving parents when his own family fractured. When he needed a job, her dad gave him one and eventually he knew the ins and outs of Cottonwood as well as she did.

Then he'd left.

"He was like a son," Dale said, fidgeting.

He'd never been like a brother in her mind. "You're cold, Dad. Go on inside."

"Evelyn, he's the only investor I trust. If Wyatt came back and agreed with your approach, I could back the plan."

Her patience snapped like a dried twig. "But your own daughter isn't good enough?" She'd regret the words tomorrow or whenever she faced him again. "Wyatt left, Dad. I stayed. *I'm here*. My blood and sweat and tears and money are invested, one hundred percent." She clamped her mouth shut before she blurted out that Wyatt was currently in town.

If her dad learned Wyatt was at the casino, gambling, he'd likely go and drag the boy out by the collar. Man. Wyatt barely resembled the boy he'd been at eighteen.

Why did she stay? She'd tried time and again to bring her father around to her way of thinking and this was just proof that he was locked in on an outdated vision for Cottonwood and the future. He wouldn't budge.

She could sympathize, to a point. When her hope-filled plans had been usurped by the facts, she'd adapted. Maybe her dad was just incapable of more adaptations. A bitter laugh erupted at the absurd unfairness of it all. Slamming open the car door, she ignored the heavy snow to come around and help her dad into the house.

In the foyer, he leaned the gun against the small table by the door. "Evie, you're my baby girl. I wanted more for you than this burden."

"I appreciate that, Dad. Truly. Maybe it's time you gave some thought to what I want. Lock up behind me and get some rest."

Despite her churning frustration and temper, she leaned in, giving him a big hug and a kiss on the cheek. As she walked out and closed the door between them, she realized she needed time to think and rest as well.

Staying at the cottage, though convenient, was out of the question. Too close to all the pressure and burdens, to use her dad's term. She needed some distance from the mess around here, some space to figure out her next step with her father and her business goals.

Pulling out her phone she called the casino and arranged for a room. After that, passing the barn, she called the sheriff's office and left a message requesting any information or updates on the break-in attempt.

In the short time she'd been off the roads, it looked as if two inches of snow had fallen. Grateful for the chains, she made it back to the casino and found a spot in the employee parking lot. As she walked in, the world seemed hushed, even the wind had gone quiet. It was just her and the snowflakes until she was inside.

The hum of energy was lower at this hour, but still present. She went to the breakroom and picked up her overnight bag before heading to the hotel area and checking in. Even when they were officially at capacity, the hotel had a few basic rooms available for emergencies like this.

Once inside, she locked the door and shrugged off her coat and boots, leaving both to drip-dry in the bathroom. She stripped off her uniform tie and vest, hanging them up on a hanger and dropped to the edge of the bed to count her tips. When the amount was logged into the app she used to track the family and business budget, she tucked the cash into a safe pocket in her purse.

She was chilled inside and out from the weather and tumultuous conversations with Wyatt and her dad. Changing into the flannel pants and thermal top she'd packed, she piled her hair on top of her head and prepared for bed.

Under the covers with the lights out, sleep proved elusive. Punching the pillow into shape she curled onto her side, blaming Wyatt for keeping her up. Thinking about him gave the whole bizarre encounter at the table and afterward too much power. He'd gone and done and lived. She might have only wandered off to college, but her accomplishments weren't *less than* his.

Flopping to her back, she stretched her feet under the covers and forced her mind to other topics. How much longer could she keep things going without an investor? Yeah, that wasn't going to help her sleep either. Outside, the wind rose on a howl and snowflakes pelted the window. It was a fitting echo for the way she felt pushed and shoved into feelings she'd thought were long gone.

Giving in, she reached for her phone on the nightstand and opened her reading app. Her best hope to silence the turmoil was to lose herself in the plight of the characters in the mystery novel she'd picked up a few days ago.

CHAPTER FOUR

On the dresser, one of Wyatt's phones started ringing. He rolled over and checked the time. He'd been in the military long enough to know nothing good happened before five a.m. With a curse, he hauled himself up and out of bed to answer.

"Jameson," he said, recognizing Agent Pickering's number.

"Open your door in five minutes. I don't want to have to knock."

He shoved a hand through his hair. "Then give me ten." After a restless night tossing and turning, he was in no condition to receive visitors. "And bring coffee." He heard her sputtering, but didn't stay on the line long enough to hear her actual reply.

Speeding through a shower, he brushed his teeth and managed to be fully dressed when his time was up. Opening the door, the FBI agent slipped inside, carrying a to-go cup of coffee in each hand.

"This is yours," she said.

She wore jeans and a black turtleneck sweater under a blazer. The heels she'd worn last night in the casino had been replaced with more practical low boots. He supposed it was an attempt to blend in. From his perspective, the guise did nothing to mute her professional, serious vibe.

"Have you looked outside?" she asked.

He accepted the cup she offered and removed the lid, inhaling the steam. "Afraid not." He paused to take a sip of the coffee before crossing to the window.

It was a winter wonderland outside and the snow was coming down straight and steady at the moment. Everything was softened by a heavy blanket of white. In the sunlight, it would sparkle, but the heavy clouds didn't look as if they planned on moving out anytime soon.

"How much of a problem does this pose?" Pickering asked.

Wyatt let the curtain fall, blocking the view. "No problem on my end." He watched her over the rim of his cup. "We might have slow going, but I'll get Cordell and his crew to the rendezvous point."

Her mouth tugged down on one side before she stilled the reaction. First sign of trouble. "What are you thinking?" he asked.

She leaned against the wall, suddenly looking as tired as he felt. "You're sure he won't delay until the weather clears?"

Wyatt took another gulp of coffee, willing the caffeine to kick in fast. "As I reported yesterday, he has a timeline and he's determined to keep it."

"The weather updates are calling for things to get much worse out there."

"And?" Blame the lack of sleep, but he was done tiptoeing around whatever she had to say.

"The order just came down." She refused to meet his gaze. "My team can't go anywhere if there's a weather advisory."

What the hell? "Are you telling me that even if I deliver Cordell on time, the FBI won't be there to catch him?"

"We'll be there if the roads are open and clear," she said.

"What does that mean?" He stopped, clamped a hand over his mouth before he started shouting. "I've told you he's going through with this robbery on schedule."

She looked up but didn't say a word. "Maybe he'll come to his senses."

Wyatt stalked back to the window. His leg ached with the incoming weather. "You came to me, remember? You tapped *me* because I'm a pro at the terrain and I know the area."

"That's right."

"And after making sure Cordell brought me into his plans, you'll leave me hanging out there, in what is sure to be a damn mess, with Cordell and his crew."

"Believe me, I want to be there. Cordell has made fools of us time and again. Last time, he killed an agent, a good friend of mine. I'm not letting him get away."

He stared at her, soaking in the explanation of her persistence in this operation. Not much consolation though if he was supposed to wrangle with Cordell alone in the middle of a blizzard.

She turned her coffee cup in her hands. "What do you know about Evelyn Cotton?"

"Everything," he answered without thinking. He might not know every single detail of her life since he'd left, but he could see that, circumstances aside, she was the same person. And his instinct to protect her hadn't dimmed a bit. "She's not connected to the robbery."

Thank goodness he'd convinced her to stay away from the casino until the storm passed.

"That's a curious opinion with no facts backing it up," Pickering challenged. "Convince me."

"You first," Wyatt countered. He sat down at the table.

Eventually she took the chair across from him. "She's had no less than three phone calls with Cordell and two online appointments he didn't keep."

"You mentioned they talked about money."

"Her family business is in serious trouble," Pickering stated. "Money trouble pushes people to take drastic measures."

"She's already doing that by dealing poker," Wyatt said, dismissing that faulty logic. "Evelyn is not a fan of the casino system."

"Because of your mother's problems."

"In part." Because she was a good friend to him at one time and back then if something hurt one of them, it hurt them both. "For Evelyn the problem with casinos is that they're indoor activities. That woman loves the fresh air and open sky. She feels caged inside and that feeling is exacerbated with schedules and requirements like clocking in and promoting an activity she doesn't believe in."

"So we should've put her into Cordell's gang instead of you."

Wyatt's jaw clenched. "You make a good point. It's possible Cordell is working up a plan B to prevent me from leading him into a trap."

"It's more likely she's in on it. Be alert."

He wouldn't allow Pickering to make him smell smoke where there wasn't any fire. "You're wrong. She isn't even in the casino and won't be until after the storm blows through."

Pickering leaned forward. "She is. After your chat, she left, apparently just long enough to get chains on her tires."

He didn't believe her. The FBI was pushing him into a corner for some unfathomable reason.

"Her car is in the employee lot," Pickering continued. "They gave her a room so she can stay and work straight through the storm."

"No." This couldn't be happening. He'd sent her out of Cordell's reach. Wyatt didn't want Evie anywhere close when the robbery went down.

"Denial never did anyone any favors," Pickering said with a slow shake of her head.

"You're wrong about her," he insisted.

She cocked her head. "I like you, Wyatt. Your military service record speaks volumes, which means I trust you. Evelyn Cotton is your blind spot."

He couldn't argue that.

"People change," Pickering continued. "They get in trouble and do rash things. Cordell baited the hook with money and she swallowed it."

He had to admit something like that was possible. "I might have a blind spot," he allowed, "but you're a pessimist operating with a bias."

The agent didn't flinch or deny it. "Experience." She held her hands wide.

"Why are you so sure you're right about a woman you've never met?" Wyatt demanded. If Evie was here, she might need an ally in law enforcement before this was over. He had to show Pickering the truth about her character. "Evelyn has lived here all her life. She's never had a speeding ticket as far as I know. You told me Cordell makes big grabs and leaves the area. Evelyn wants to stay in Deadwood. She always has."

"Desperate people do desperate things. He calls himself an investor, she probably hasn't bothered to figure out where the man gets his money, she just needs the cash. Happens all the time."

Wyatt scrubbed at his whiskers. "You're wrong. And when you figure it out, I hope you accept your mistake and do right by her."

"Blind spot," she muttered under her breath. "The two of you aren't kids anymore. You have no idea what she's capable of now."

"And you do?" Wyatt was ready to toss Agent Pickering

and her FBI pals and the big payday right out of his room. "Cordell is the problem," he insisted. "Not Evelyn."

"Aside from the money she needs, there's the matter of a dead security guard they found downstairs an hour after she checked in."

"This entire endeavor has turned into a nightmare." The premise had been tricky enough to start with. He shoved away from the table. "I suppose you have Evelyn gamely smiling into a security camera near the scene. Naturally, you suspect her."

"She was in the building and she knows the layout and placement of all the security measures. We are monitoring the situation while the local authorities work the case."

She was pulling his chain to get a reaction. Fine. He could play that game, having learned from the best gamers in the military chain of command. "What details do you have?"

"We are monitoring the situation," she repeated pointedly.

"You're crazy if you think she's capable of murder." He could walk away, he'd done it before and landed on his feet. So what if he was a little lame on one side. There were better ways to get his business off the ground. "You're looking at this all wrong."

"Again, I'm open to clarification and insight."

She wasn't. Cordell was Pickering's blind spot and now, with Evie, the federal agent was a junkyard dog with a fresh bone. "You trust me?"

"Within reason," she allowed.

"Then trust me vouching for her. Evelyn is not a killer. She is not a criminal of any sort. Her interactions with Cordell are all on *him*." Wyatt stalked over and drilled a finger to the tabletop. "She is the most honest, reliable, and genuine person I've ever known. And I can guarantee if she gave her word to be somewhere, she wouldn't let weather stop her."

Pickering flinched. "Noted."

"I want your word that if I get Cordell to the rendezvous and you're not there, I still get paid."

Her lip curled. "You'll get paid when he's in custody."

It was clearly the best he'd get from her right now. "If he comes to his senses and delays his plan, I'll let you know."

Pickering walked out of his room, leaving him antsy and frustrated. Evie was in the casino and a guard was dead. Wyatt scrubbed at his face. Please let that be an accident of some sort. According to Cordell's schedule all of the people and pieces should've been in place by last night and taking out a guard wasn't on the agenda.

And Evie had gone home for chains and returned to the casino.

No, that had to be a coincidence. He did *not* want Pickering to be right about her. Or about his blind spot. But there was no reason for her to help Cordell commit this robbery. The diamonds, on display in the jewelry store, weren't even close to the poker room. No reason for Cordell to need Evie's car, with or without chains on the tires. Baker and Karl were the trusted members of Cordell's team. Baker would drive the getaway car. Wyatt was the navigator.

He would focus. He'd stay alert. And, as much as he wanted to, he absolutely would *not* track her down and ask her outright about Cordell.

That kind of mistake would be mission suicide on all fronts. He checked his watch. Next up for him was one last casino walk in a few hours. Pickering's coffee chat was an effective reminder that the FBI would be watching him even more closely, along with Karl, if not Cordell himself.

Once that was complete, the twenty-four countdown to the robbery would begin.

EVELYN OPENED THE CURTAINS, a little stunned by the amount of snow that had fallen in the few hours she'd slept. It was still coming down, though the wind didn't look so bad right now.

Thank goodness she'd been smart and come back last night. Not even chains would've gotten her out of her driveway today. If the clouds were any indication, conditions would worsen all day long. She used the in-room coffee pot for her first kick of caffeine and turned on the television for an update on road conditions while it brewed. A news reporter was outside, snow gathering along her shoulder and hood as she urged people to stay home.

Evelyn picked up her phone, her thumb hovering over the icon to call her dad. She just couldn't do it. He was safe at home, with all the supplies he needed to ride out the storm. They could pick up their argument where they left off when the storm was over.

"Wyatt," she muttered to the empty room. Her father would have to adjust his fantasy and learn to trust her judgment. Wyatt was not going to miraculously bail them out.

It stung, like wind-driven icy rain against her cheeks, the way her father resisted good ideas. He wouldn't be impressed about her finalizing the sledding day for the hospitality team-builder. Maybe she should talk to Tate about a private loan to buy her father out of the business. Then Dale could retire and she could expand, intelligently, until Cottonwood Adventures was as much a destination in Deadwood as the Silver Aces.

None of her problems would be solved today. Her shift started in a few hours and she planned to do some yoga before breakfast. She needed the mental and physical reset before turning on the tip-magnet charm at the poker table. Especially on a day when the weather would drastically reduce their business.

Half-way through the warm-up her phone buzzed. She ignored it at first, assuming it was the normal report on guests, gambling volume, and players to watch. When the buzzing kept up, she paused to check. There were text messages from her manager and another general broadcast from casino security, along with responses from a few friends on staff.

She stared at the messages, switching back and forth, reading and rereading them. One of the guards had been found dead a few hours ago. The victim's name wasn't provided, but she counted several people on that team as her friends. The entire staff was being asked to cooperate with the law enforcement agencies investigating the situation.

She couldn't wrap her head around it. Things like this didn't happen here. The casinos in Deadwood dealt with their fair share of crime, but finding bodies wasn't common. Fights. Petty theft, shoplifting, grifters. Those were the things the casino trained them to watch out for.

Giving up on yoga and forgetting breakfast, Evie showered and dressed for her upcoming shift. Taking only her cell phone and room key, she headed downstairs to figure out how she could help. If she could help.

The typical calm in the employee area had shifted to a solemn quiet this morning. Everyone was subdued. She stepped aside as a team of detectives passed her, escorted by Sheriff Russell.

The sheriff paused and urged the detectives to go on without him. "Evelyn."

"Yes, sir?" She looked up into the tall man's weathered face and suddenly felt better. He had a calming, confident effect, which was one reason why he kept getting re-elected.

"Is your dad all right?" he asked. "I didn't expect to see you here today."

She smiled. "Dad's fine. I went home last night to get the

tire chains and came back rather than take a chance that I couldn't get here for my shift today. He told me about the break in."

"Did you look around?"

"Yes. I didn't see anything missing."

"Glad to hear it. I planned to drop in and take a closer look in the daylight but with the storm and now this, ah..."

She saved him from finishing that sentence. "Dad's fine out there," she assured him. The last thing she wanted was to think about a dead body in the building. "I can't imagine anyone will give us any more trouble while the snow is coming down like this."

"Fingers crossed, you're right. It'll be white-out conditions soon. You're riding it out here?" When she nodded, he excused himself. Stopping short, he turned back. "Did you check in before four a.m.?"

"Yes," she replied immediately. "The front desk will have the exact time."

"Good, good. And did you go anywhere besides your room or leave your room at all after you checked in?"

"Not until a few minutes ago when I came down here to help," she replied.

He jotted her answers in his memo pad and tucked it back in his shirt pocket. "Be careful in the poker room today. The people who didn't get out are bound to get a little stir crazy." With a sad smile, he hurried after the detectives. She didn't envy him at all.

In the breakroom, Sarah caught up with her immediately. "It was Stan," her manager said quietly. "He...he died from a head injury."

Evelyn sank into the nearest chair as her knees gave out. She thought of Stan's wife and the baby who would never know his dad. "Someone attacked him?"

Sarah glanced around. "They don't know the whole story

yet, Evie," she said with heart-wrenching sympathy. "I know the two of you were friends."

"Was anyone here *not* friends with him?" Stan was that kind of approachable, the friendliest kind of guy willing to lend a hand if you needed to move a couch or needed help with a flat tire. She'd known him since high school, though he'd been two years ahead of her. "Stupid question," she said. "The detectives wouldn't be here if it was an accident."

Sarah shushed her. "We don't want to speculate or raise more rumors," she scolded softly. "Can you take your shift today or do you need to go home?"

Evie pulled herself together. "I'll be fine by the time I'm needed on the floor. It's not like I could get out of here if I wanted to."

"We won't be at capacity," her manager said. "If you get overwhelmed, just say the word and we'll adjust."

"I appreciate that, but busy is better for me right now." She looked around at the others milling about in the break-room. "What can I do to help you?"

Sarah pursed her lips. "Are you feeling creative? We have about seventy-five conference attendees who didn't make it to the airport before the runway closed."

"I thought evacuations were yesterday." It still blew her mind that it had become an issue.

Evie had never seen such a panic around a storm. The Black Hills and all of the businesses in and around Deadwood had been coping with weather events since forever. She knew her disappointment was more about losing out on tips. Dumb and completely the wrong priority, especially in lieu of Stan's death.

"They hemmed and hawed and then it was too late," Sarah said with a shrug. "Can you help me organize a couple of poker tournaments? The hotel is comping some spa packages, but that won't appeal to everyone."

Evie could organize a rafting or hiking trip in about fifteen minutes flat and she worked this problem with a similar mental checklist. It was a matter of number of people involved, skill levels and interests, along with location options. "I assume you'll want to keep this out of the main poker room?" she asked.

"Definitely. We'll use the ballroom. Plenty of room to set up several tables."

"Got it." Evie was thinking about the numbers. "What about dealers?"

"If you're willing to take the lead, I can shuffle staff around to make it work."

She was more than willing to work in an area where Wyatt wouldn't see her. It would be almost as good as keeping her promise to stay home until the storm passed. She had no reason to feel guilty breaking her word, especially not with him, but old habits die hard.

"Then I'll get on it. This is a great idea," Evie added as she stood up. Her knees were steady again and she was filled with purpose, relieved to focus on something other than her dead friend and her problems at home.

"Fabulous," Sarah said. "Head over to hospitality and they'll help you get everything in place."

Her new focus failed her as soon as she entered the casino floor, mindful that Wyatt could be out here too. How long would he be in town? She hadn't asked because knowing how many more chances she had to run into him was dangerous. A gamble. He'd said he loved her and she believed he did care. Or had once cared.

Didn't matter. Aside from her father, Wyatt was the only man in her life with the ability to hurt her. Deeply. He'd done it once and she couldn't give him room to do it again.

She wasn't proud of herself for cutting off typical relationships. As if anyone else would have a chance while she was still hung up on him. It was embarrassing really, and probably why she didn't talk about it. Eleven years really should be enough time to get over her high school 'sweetheart'. Acceptance was the first step toward full recovery. The sooner she accepted that she'd never worked through her feelings for Wyatt, the sooner she could move on. For real this time.

And what if he stayed in Deadwood? He said he looked you up.

She cut off that annoying little voice in a hurry. It was bad enough that Wyatt was in town, and worse that he was staying in a casino. Her casino. Whatever crazy twist of fate that brought him back into her sphere was irrelevant.

But if he planned to stay...

Her imagination hijacked basic logic. They might rekindle their friendship, he might convince her father to take a chance on *her* plans. And pigs might soon be flying through the blizzard bearing down on the area.

She couldn't count on Wyatt's plans or anyone else's. Her goals and ideas took precedence. She was sufficient and capable and... and still hopelessly hung up on a man who'd broken her heart.

Annoyed with herself, she clutched her phone, lifted her chin and thought about the seventy-five people who would soon be wandering around searching for distraction and entertainment.

Turning down the hall to the hospitality office, she almost plowed into Jack Thornton, a hospitality manager on the guest relations side the Silver Aces operation. He caught her shoulders and steadied her.

"Hello, Evelyn." His eyes roamed over her face and his hands withdrew slowly. "We heard what happened. Are you okay?"

"Yeah, um, thanks." He'd asked her out last week. His dark hair and eyes made him pretty much the opposite of Wyatt, but he was fit and friendly and had only been in Deadwood for five years or so. There was no lumpy, old emotional baggage between them. Suddenly she couldn't recall why she'd turned him down. "Sarah sent me over for the ballroom set up."

Jack's eyes lit up. "So we'll be working together today?"

"Looks like it." A pleasant sensation swept through her as she smiled back at him. This *would* be a great day. "I was thinking—" An alert made her phone vibrate in her hands. "One second."

She skimmed the email message quickly and a happy cheer burst free, startling Jack. "Sorry." Finally, Tate Cordell had reached out. From the tone of the email, he'd made a decision to invest in Cottonwood, despite not seeing the area firsthand. She pressed her lips together hard to keep from squealing with joy while she dashed off a reply.

This was exactly the kind of investment she needed to elevate the family business and provide tours and services year-round. According to the email, the package she'd sent with testimonials and proposals, along with her thorough business plan impressed him. The number he provided as his initial funding was twice the total she'd hoped to secure and he asked when and where he could wire the funds. Right now worked for her, if only so she could ogle the bigger bank balance online until the storm passed. She sent him the details for the wire transfer.

"Evelyn, are you all right?"

"I am!" She hooked her arm in Jack's and did a quick do-si-do turn in the hallway. "I just got the *best* news."

"Well, you certainly deserve that," he said.

"Thanks." She knew he didn't mean it as a downer, but out of respect for Stan, she dialed down her celebration. "Let's get going," she said. "I've been working on some long-term solutions for the family business," she explained as they took the service hallway to the ballroom. "It looks like it's all finally coming together."

"I'm happy for you," Jack said. "Cottonwood is a great enterprise."

He couldn't have offered a more perfect response. "Thank you."

In the ballroom they quickly formed a plan to give the stranded conference attendees a decent place to hang out, play for low to zero stakes, and network. "They might as well get more than they came for," Evie said.

Jack walked over to the corner to the right of the doors. "We'll keep beverage service and a buffet going in this corner. Games over there," he pointed to the opposite corner.

"Sure thing. I'm thinking with this size group, we only need three poker tables and two for black jack." They discussed the rest of the layout and tables for mingling. "You have enough wait staff."

"We're compressing services across the board. It'll work." He planted his hands on his hips. "Do you really think we'll get six feet of snow?"

She glanced up from the update she was sending to her manager. "Are you afraid of cabin fever setting in?"

"More like a power outage," he admitted, pulling out his own phone. "According to this update, the preliminary stage of this storm ends just after noon today and we'll be in the thick of it."

"Come on, Jack. You know the casino is prepared for any crisis."

"Sure." His gaze moved to the doors. "I just don't like the idea of being snowed in."

"Trust me, if it's half as bad as they're predicting, you'll be happier inside than out." She was still floating high on the knowledge that her business had been saved to worry about weather or stir-crazy customers. "Now that we know how many tables, I'll go get what we need. Think we can open to the group around ten?"

Jack nodded absently while he keyed details into his phone, presumably passing along the schedule and information to his staff.

She practically floated out of the ballroom, the smile on her face a permanent fixture as she crossed the casino. It was remarkable how quickly her concerns and frustrations evaporated. One email promising money and she positively glowed inside and out. Her mind gleefully ran the numbers from modest to bold to outrageous, prioritizing her expansion plans. Thanks to various marketing podcasts and years in the local outdoor-adventure industry, she could justify each and every change she planned to make. Neither her father nor her new investor would have cause to doubt or worry.

It was nearly noon when members of the stranded group started meandering into their private casino floor. In general, they seemed distracted by the gloomy weather reports and the blanket of white outside every hotel room window. Evie mingled. There was no reason to take her station as dealer yet. She made suggestions and asked questions, polling the guests on everything from how the Silver Aces could make the impromptu stay better to their favorite winter activities.

They wouldn't have thought of it yet, but once Holly was done and gone, it would take time for roads to clear and airports to reopen. How much time was solely dependent on the amount of snow Holly unleashed. On another quick errand behind the scenes, Evie caught a glimpse of the near white-out conditions through a window. It was easier to understand Jack's earlier concern. She made a mental note to brainstorm ideas that would keep people busy and engaged once the sun came out again.

"Evie? What are you doing here?"

She cringed at the sound of Wyatt's voice, but she did

stop to speak to him politely. "I could ask you the same thing." Her pulse kicked at the sight of him. Why couldn't she enjoy this same flutter when she looked at Jack? Or any other man?

"Don't do that," he said. "You promised me you'd be at home today."

She guided him to the nearest alcove and tried to give him a genuine smile. It faltered. "I work here, Wyatt. This is where I'm needed, especially with a storm that's closing roads. Why didn't you get out last night?"

"I told you I'm here on business." He frowned, his gaze roaming the space again.

"Same for me." She gave a small shrug, thinking about her investor. "Besides I'm local," she quipped, her happiness still fizzing through her. She was a local and thanks to Tate she'd remain a local business owner. "And I'm on the schedule."

"I suggested leaving yesterday morning and was shot down." His frown didn't ease much. "This morning I told my boss it was too late to get out," he said. "I'll catch a flight after the storm."

"You had time to change hotels." He couldn't possibly want to spend more time in a casino than necessary.

"Maybe I was hoping to run into you again. I'd like more time with you."

His voice tempted her to believe, to entertain the possibility of something more between them than awkward, lingering feelings. Suddenly, she was swept back to their last summer as Cottonwood guides and the sweet summer-infused kisses they shared down by the creek. Nothing awkward about those kisses. He'd smelled of sunshine, his hair lightened and his skin bronzed from hours in the sun. Her gaze dropped to his lips and she caught herself before she foolishly leaned in for a fresh taste of him.

"Are you implying you knew I'd come back to the casino?" she asked, folding her arms to hold herself back.

His expression eased, mischief dancing in his blue eyes. Her stomach twirled in response, as if she was going over that first, thrilling plunge on a roller coaster. Why couldn't she resist him?

"Goes to show I still know my best friend. Can I take you to lunch?" he offered.

"No, thank you." She had to hang on to her resolve. He was talking about friendship and her heart and hormones were screaming for something else entirely. Wyatt was her past. Her future was the casino and Cottonwood thanks to Tate. "We're on a skeleton staff and I need to get back."

She continued back to the ballroom and he followed her inside. "This is...wait. What is this?" he asked.

"A special event. Private for this particular group," she replied. "They're stranded until the storm passes." She saw the queue for waiting poker players and, smiling, walked to the open table where she would be running an introductory game of Texas Hold 'em. "You really can't be here."

Again, he trailed after her. "You thought of this," he said as the players took their seats.

She shot him a warning look as a few guests took chairs around the table. "The Silver Aces was happy to find a way to make the weather less of an inconvenience for our guests."

"We're glad you did," one woman said. Her hair was gray and she had laugh lines at her eyes and a speculative smile as her gaze moved between Evie and Wyatt. "Will you join us, handsome?"

"I'm afraid Mr. Jameson is on his way out."

"Evie, I just want five more minutes." His phone rang and he glared at the screen before declining the call.

"That's Miss Cotton," she corrected him with no heat at all. What a difference a little bit of hope could make. She wasn't as scared of what she might do or say. Of the fallout if she did something impulsive. The email from Tate had infused her with confidence and a subtle affirmation that things were moving in the right direction. Finally. "He's an old friend," she explained to the players gathered around the table.

"When is your break?" Wyatt pressed.

"You need to stop." She removed the deck from the automatic shuffler. "I have plans over my break."

The older woman with the laugh lines eyed Wyatt again and bobbed her eyebrows. "In your shoes, honey, I'd adjust the schedule."

Evie chuckled. "He's always been persistent." She was too relieved to be overly irritated by Wyatt. "Now, let's talk about the game."

Wyatt pulled up a chair and she chose to ignore him. If he kept quiet, no one would notice him and she could escort him out during her break. She gave a preliminary overview to the group and they followed along, asking intelligent questions as they worked through the opening bets and rounds of the game.

She'd almost forgotten he was there until the lesson was over and the other players wandered off to other activities. "I'll walk you out."

He frowned at his phone again before shoving it into his pocket. "Will you be here all night?" he asked. "In here, I mean."

"Yes." She told herself his obsession with her schedule didn't matter. It wasn't romantic or flattering, just an old friend keeping tabs. Probably out of boredom as much as nostalgia. "And you need to *not* be in here."

"Fine." His brow furrowed and he reached out, his fingers a whisper along her jaw. "I just wish you were home in front of a big fire with a mug of hot chocolate."

"Me too." It's how they'd waited out more than one storm as kids. Something was troubling him, but it was too soon to resume her role as the person who gave him a place to vent and talk out his worries. "If you're still in town after the storm passes, you should come to the house for dinner. Dad would love to see you."

He perked up. "I'll hold you to that, Evie."

She expected no less. As he walked off, she realized she wasn't nearly as afraid of that dinner anymore. All of the hostility and insecurity she'd felt yesterday had faded and she wanted to stay on this happier ground.

Oh, what a difference an investor made.

CHAPTER FIVE

WYATT BARELY GOT around the corner before his temper kicked into high gear. He'd received text messages from Agent Pickering and Cordell, along with alerts from the National Weather Service.

At least the NWS didn't expect anything from him.

He reviewed the last three messages from Pickering, all of them relating to Evie's ties to Cordell. The agent needed to back off, but it clearly wasn't going to happen. Keeping in mind the reward the FBI promised him, he returned to his room.

Pickering was waiting. "I don't even want to address how you got in here," he grumbled.

"Good. Address this instead." She opened a laptop and turned the screen to face him. "Cordell just promised your old pal ten thousand dollars. Hours after a casino guard is found dead."

"Coincidence."

Pickering swore. "The sheriff and detectives dismissed her as a suspect," she said. "They'll change their minds when we give them this. It's an obvious payoff."

"I hate Deadwood," Wyatt muttered, stalking to the window. He never should've come anywhere close to home. It was a black hole that sucked at his soul. The only bright spot had been Evie and now, thanks to him, somehow Cordell and the FBI had fixed on her. "If anyone had saved her business, she wouldn't have come in today."

"She had to be here to kill the guard and earn that business-saving payout." Pickering sneered. "If you can't see that, you might want to rethink your plans as an investigator."

"Same to you," he snapped. "Evie is not the killer. Whatever Cordell is up to, it's about the robbery. The only business he's interested in is his own."

Wyatt was running out of time to figure out what Cordell would gain by dragging Evie into this online, or in person. He showed Pickering the texts from Cordell on the burner phone stating the robbery would go down at seven p.m. tonight.

"You have to keep him in the building," she said.

"The plan is to drive away, to the rendezvous. That's why you gave me the GPS tracker."

"Have you looked outside? The conditions will be impassable by then. It's perfect. You can keep him in the building."

"How?"

"Use your friend," Pickering suggested. "She knows where to hide, how to navigate around cameras."

"That's a tragedy waiting to happen." There was no telling what Cordell might do, who he might hurt if he felt cornered.

"The guard's death makes sense now," Pickering said. She was practically glowing with excitement. "One less person on staff. He'll use that gap."

"A gap interrupted by a casino crawling with a sheriff and detectives. If Cordell did set up that guard, he's a fool."

"But he thinks it's only local law enforcement. He's overconfident. Wyatt, I've studied him and I can tell you he studied the area and the resources. He brought you on because of your experience."

"You set that up. Made me look like the right man for his crew." He regretted reaching out to ask that favor of his pal from the Army. They probably should've tapped someone like Evie, someone far more familiar with the area than he was after eleven years away. He wasn't about to say so.

"Use your friend," Pickering repeated. "We can end this tonight."

Wyatt shook his head. "She's busy working a private event. I can't pester her."

Pickering scowled. "If you don't use her, Cordell will. Get ready for that. Better if you can turn her before this goes down."

The warning just hit him all wrong. "Enough. I'm doing what you asked." He stalked out of his hotel room and down the hall. He'd hold up his end with the FBI, but it was less about the reward and more about making sure Evie didn't get caught in the snare intended for Cordell.

Furious, with himself and the situation he'd lost control of, he stalked all the way to the casino's front door. The depth of the snow stopped him even before the uniformed guard could remind him he'd want a coat before stepping outside.

"Valet service is closed, sir."

"Looks like a good idea," Wyatt said. "The doors are operational, right?"

"Of course." The guard puffed out his chest. "Fire code demands it."

"Has to be three feet deep already," Wyatt murmured.

"Yes, sir. And counting. Next update is noon, but I don't expect to hear that Holly has turned away."

Wyatt had to agree. "Can I step out on the portico if I promise not to wander away?"

"I can't actually force you to stay inside, sir. Please use the side door rather than the slider." He gestured to the single door at the far side of the automatic doors.

"Sure" Wyatt agreed. "No need to turn both of us into popsicles."

"Much appreciated."

Outside Wyatt took a deep breath, regretting it instantly. The frigid air was like inhaling icicles. Despite that, the stillness, the utter quiet, was refreshing. No sounds of traffic or exuberant people coming and going. A man could feel alone out here.

And a thief carrying millions of dollars worth of diamonds could get lost and freeze to death in a hurry. He waited for any sound of plows or salt trucks working the highway. Now the silence worried him. He knew they wouldn't run constantly, but he expected them to run. Maybe the guard inside would know the schedule.

Standing here, his feet and hands chilled through, Wyatt understood why the FBI refused to grant their agents permission to travel in these conditions. If he had any hope of getting Cordell, his men and the loot into Pickering's custody, he had to be the driver. Baker didn't have enough experience with these roads, he wouldn't know how to navigate the unseen dangers in these conditions.

Wyatt walked to the edge of the portico that some poor employee was trying to keep clear and swiped his hand through a drift to get a feel for the snow's texture. Heavy and wet. Snow like this would weigh down tree limbs and power lines, add in ice when the peak winds set in and they were in for one helluva risky drive out of Deadwood.

"The odds are not in our favor," he whispered into the falling snow.

He had to convince Cordell to wait. Moving today was suicide. Wyatt hadn't survived his mother's antics, his father's denial, or an improvised explosive in Afghanistan just to throw his life away here. Not for the sake of justice or his fledgling business. And Evie had just opened the door for them to reconnect. If he died out here, the FBI wouldn't bother to clear his name. No amount of reward money was worth the risk that Evie would believe he was on the wrong side of the law with Cordell's crew.

He walked back toward the door, halting when the Cordell phone buzzed. The two words on the screen left him shell-shocked. One hour.

One hour? No way. The countdown had been adjusted once already. He scrambled to reply and thanks to his chilled hands, he bobbled the phone. Fortunately, the snow caught it before any real damage could be done.

He shoved it inside a pocket, his heart racing. This was a huge mistake.

"You okay, sir?"

"It's brisk," he said, trying to pin his reaction on the weather. "Take care, man." He hurried deeper into the casino, taking momentary refuge at a slot machine. What the hell was Cordell thinking? Juggling the plan like this was dangerous.

Granted, Wyatt wasn't an expert in the field of jewel theft. Pretty much the opposite. He'd been working his way through the ranks in as an Army MP when the injury ended his career. The FBI had given him plenty of background on Tate Cordell, touting him as one of the best when it came to parting stores from their priceless gems. So far, the man wasn't living up to Wyatt's idea of an elusive criminal mastermind.

Several replies dashed through Wyatt's mind, none of which he entered into the phone. Tate didn't want advice or opinions. He expected full cooperation from everyone, including Wyatt who was only here to guide them north to the rendezvous point in a ghost town where another driver would be waiting to help them escape.

Except Wyatt's job was to make sure the FBI was in place well ahead of the rendezvous time so they could gather up Tate, Baker, and Karl along with the driver waiting in the ghost town. And the FBI was definitely not going out in the teeth of the storm. Still, he sent the required text update to Pickering.

The rendezvous point, less than ten miles away, was an intermediate level cross-country hike in good weather. The drive could take over an hour on the twisting two-lane road on a clear day. In these treacherous conditions there was no way to give an accurate estimate on drive time. If the road was even passable.

They'd find out for sure soon enough. He should probably be happy this entire mess would be over sooner rather than later. Wyatt couldn't muster enough relief to smother the trepidation.

With precisely forty-five minutes to the robbery, he moved into position, following the plan Cordell had assigned him. He entered the casual dining restaurant, grateful it was still open, and sat down at a table closest to the gaming floor. He ordered a cup of coffee and waited.

Baker and Karl would be close, though Wyatt hadn't spotted them yet.

His coffee arrived and he thanked the waitress. The only bright spot was that Evie was out of sight, working in that ballroom and nowhere near the retail area. She wouldn't see him commit a crime. He couldn't help wondering if she'd believe it when the casino security linked him to the robbery. She'd have to when they showed her the camera feed. Despite Cordell's plans, it would be impossible to avoid every camera.

He could already imagine Sheriff Russell interrogating her about Wyatt and their recent conversations in and around the casino. If he wasn't already double-crossing Cordell, knowing Evie would suffer would be enough to turn him against the thief.

She would hate him for the rest of her life. What he was about to do would not only make the FBI take a harder look at her finances and her recent ties to Cordell, it would likely cost her the job here at the Silver Aces. He pinched the bridge of his nose. She'd take some heat from the community too, not unlike some of the griping aimed at her because she spent so much time with him, the only son of the woman who owed money to everyone in town.

Somehow, if he got Cordell's crew into FBI custody, Wyatt would find a way to make it up to her.

Playing his assigned role, he sipped his coffee and kept his gaze on his phone. Bringing up the weather app, he nearly swore out loud. The radar showed the entire area covered by thick bands of snow and icy precipitation. Cordell must be trying to get the diamonds out ahead of the road closures. If he'd bothered to ask before throwing all of this into motion, Wyatt could've explained why that wouldn't work.

He used the app to zoom out, looking for a better way from Deadwood to the rendezvous. Heading south first might be the best hope of making it within a day. The only good news was that the law enforcement, sure to follow them, would have an equal challenge. His stomach knotted. Law enforcement who gave chase would also run the risk of driving right off the road.

Opening the text messages, he sent a private message to Cordell, suggesting he postpone the robbery.

Cordell: Cold feet?

Wyatt: Common sense. Move the meet.

Cordell: Meet stays. Contact is out of reach.

Wyatt: Understood.

Great. This was going down, weather be damned. He

considered warning Cordell that the route might shift, but didn't bother. He watched the minutes tick down on the clock displayed on his phone. Right on time, Tate Cordell strolled by the restaurant, crossing from the slot machines toward the retail row of shops. It was the first time Wyatt had seen him here at the casino and he looked for all the world like a man without a care.

Wyatt fought back a sudden urge to blow up the entire plan. Sure it would cost him his reward money but Evie wouldn't hate him. With one text or an anonymous phone call, he could tip off the casino security staff. A trickle of dread slid down his spine as he considered it. Upping the timeline, trying to stick with the same escape route in this weather was all wrong.

With twenty minutes to go, he received a reminder from Pickering that local support was officially suspended for weather, followed by a suggestion to keep Cordell and his crew in the building.

Sure, because a standoff in a building that couldn't be evacuated would be so much more appealing than an escape through a blizzard. Was the snow impairing everyone's common sense?

He sat back, a picture of calm when he wanted to jump on the table and scream out his frustrations. That was tempting, another action that would bring in security from all sides. Of course, if he did that, Cordell would use the distraction to his advantage and Wyatt would be left twisting in the wind trying to explain his breakdown to the FBI.

Nearby one of the slots paid out, complete with flashing lights, bells and music, and the coveted sound of tokens overflowing the tray. Hooray for payday, he thought, thoroughly disgusted. His mother had craved that singular, raucous sound over everything else, including food, water, and her only child. She'd chased that ultimate mood lifter, heedless of what went undone or unsaid.

With only ten minutes to go, Wyatt scanned the area, confirming the security teams were where they needed to be. He dropped cash on the table to cover his coffee, though he gave serious thought to charging it to the room. That option too would've given him a way to write a note and warn someone outside the FBI that a robbery was about to occur. Instead, he stuck with the plan, even though the FBI had suddenly withdrawn their tactical support.

He took up his new position in a seating area between the retail space and their intended exit. His expression neutral, he kept his gaze on his cell phone and waited for the alarm to sound.

"Wyatt?"

At the sound of Evie's voice, his mind blanked. This could not be happening. She was supposed to be in the ballroom. If he doubted it before, here was confirmation that the operation was cursed.

"I thought you were busy with the private event." Too busy to have lunch with him.

"What's wrong?" Her smile faded as she studied his face. "You look more upset than you did earlier." She bit her lip. "It's being here, isn't it? And now you're stuck." She turned him toward the hotel. "Come on. I can get you set up with a massage."

"No, Evie. Wait."

"On the house," she said.

He dug in his heels, blocking her view of the jewelry store and preventing her from dragging him out of position. In his head he swore a blue streak in Cordell's general direction. "You should get back to the ballroom. Don't want to miss any good tippers."

"It's less of a priority," she said. "Between you and me, Cottonwood just hit the jackpot."

"I beg your pardon?" Pickering could not be right about Evie.

"An investor reached out with a generous offer that will let me get things back on track."

"Who? How much?"

"That's not your business."

He checked his phone. In less than three minutes alarms would sound, his life would fall apart. "You should've come to me." He tried to steer her toward the ballroom, out of harm's way.

She crossed her arms over her chest. "Now you sound like my father."

It aggravated him that she'd gone to someone else for help. That she'd had to. Part of him was sure that should be his job, despite walking out on that role eleven years ago. Any second now she'd find out that her investor was a fraud, using her for... well, Wyatt wasn't sure yet.

"Did you vet this person? Have you met or drawn up contracts?"

Her gray eyes blazed with temper. "Mr. Jameson, please excuse me. Enjoy your stay at Silver Aces."

He didn't want her to leave angry, he just needed her out of the way. The flash of relief that she was gone evaporated as she turned toward the sudden shouting match behind him.

What was Cordell doing? The robbery should've gone off without any kind of shouting, only a standard alarm. He turned toward the noise, tucking Evie behind him as the glass door fronting the jewelry store exploded in a rain of sparkling shards. Also, not part of the plan.

The alarm sounded and Cordell, Baker, and Karl appeared, their boots crunching on the mess, grinding the glass against the marble floor as they hustled his way. The uniformed guard wasn't anywhere in sight, but the two plain-clothes guards were in pursuit and pulling their guns.

"Stop them," Evie said, pushing at his back.

He stepped into their path as he tried to shove Evie back and out of the way. He had to distance himself from her while still holding up his end of the exit plan.

Behind the trio of robbers, one of the men raised his gun and took a stand. "Freeze! Casino security!"

Cordell kept moving and the calculating grin on his face sent a chill over Wyatt's skin. "A hostage, smart move."

Damn it, Tate was right. It was the only safe play. As the three men passed by, he fell in behind them, dragging Evie along. He did his best not to hurt her, but he had to restrain her and make it convincing.

"Wy...att—"

She couldn't get the words out well with his forearm across her throat. "Cooperate, Miss Cotton," he said in her ear. "Cooperate and this goes easier for all of us."

He eased the pressure at her throat, but kept her arm pinned behind her back, steering her movement. The guards hesitated, barking at each other and at them, but Wyatt knew they wouldn't shoot and risk hurting her. Caution was the standard procedure when a civilian was in the way.

Cordell, in the lead, pushed open the door and cold air struck Wyatt hard as he walked backward out of the building, Evie secure in his arms. Snow swirled through the air, blurring the visibility within a few feet. Over the wind, he heard car doors opening and the roar of an engine. Baker must have double-parked the SUV close to the door. Amateur move for a supposedly professional crew. The casino security staff would have full details on the car before the crew made it to the highway.

He tried to release Evie, determined to push her back toward the guards and the safety of the casino, but Karl, who easily had fifty pounds on Wyatt, manhandled him and then Evie into the back seat and then blocked her in.

Wyatt started to drag her right on through the opposite door of the vehicle, but Cordell was there, gun in hand, blocking the move and watching him with a cocky grin. At this range Cordell wouldn't miss, even with the snow. With a split-second to decide, Wyatt stayed the course, playing his role as part of the crew. The part that took the hostage.

DEADWOOD 5 NEWS

"Joyce Adams will walk us through the latest update."

"Thanks, Will." Joyce picked up the cue from behind the weather desk. "Anyone in our viewing area only needs to look outside to see Winter Storm Holly's arrival. Some places are already reporting white-out conditions."

She cued up a radar view. "The National Weather Service midday update shows us right in the teeth of this storm. Snowfall will continue all day and well into this evening. Visibility will worsen and temperatures will drop even more tonight. When that happens, we can expect a layer of ice on top of this heavy snow."

Changing the map, she shared the latest snowfall measurements. "You can see these darker bands are where we'll see the most accumulation. We are looking at breaking weather records over the next twenty-four hours.

"Please, everyone, stay inside and stay warm. As Trooper Bob said during our morning broadcast, there is no reason to be outside or on the roads right now. Snow plows are attempting to keep up on the primary routes and even so, black ice is already a serious factor."

She smiled into the camera. "Thank you to everyone sending in pictures and video." On cue, the slides cycled through. Snow blanketed trees and rooflines and it was already impossible to differentiate between sidewalks and streets. "You can see drifts forming already in some areas. I can assure you there will be plenty of time for snowmen and forts once the storm passes."

She switched to a map showing wind speeds and wind chill. "My recommendation? Enjoy some hot chocolate by the fire. Wait until the temperatures come up a bit tomorrow afternoon before venturing out to enjoy this white wonderland Holly leaves behind.

"Will, back to you."

CHAPTER SIX

EVIE WANTED to scream and yet didn't want to give Wyatt the satisfaction. She was caught in the back seat of an SUV, with no idea what the hell was going on. She'd been talking with Wyatt one minute and then he'd used her as a shield. Against men with guns. A howl built in her throat, fighting to break free.

Behind them there was more shouting and she could barely make out the casino security team hesitating near the doors. The man near the front passenger door fired his gun, the horrible sound cracking through the blowing wind. She looked up, afraid of the worst, but she didn't see blood or any sign that the bullets had hit any of the men.

"Let me out! Let me go, please." She hated begging, but she had to get out of here before they were off casino property. "Please, Wyatt." The big SUV rolled forward and she scrambled to climb over him, but he pushed her back down. She kicked at the man behind her as he climbed in and closed the door, but he barely noticed.

"So you do know each other," the man up front said. "I thought you might." To the driver, he gave the order to go.

"Please let me out," she said again.

Wyatt was a criminal. She was trapped in a car full of criminals. She forced herself to note details of the strangers so she could give the police an accurate description whenever she got out of this. The driver, with his pale blond buzz cut, chapped cheeks, and square face reminded her of one of those cross-country skiers from Norway. Except she quickly realized he couldn't drive in the snow. The man beside her was bulky and bigger than Wyatt. He had a pleasant, but forgettable face and his dark brown hair was short, not unlike any number of businessmen who sat down at her table for a game of poker.

This couldn't be happening. Of all the wicked curve balls life had thrown at her, this was the most insulting. The most inexplicable. The absurdity sank in and she fought back with all the steel she could muster. "Let me out," she demanded, her tone flat and calm.

Up front, the man in charge buckled his seatbelt. Twisting around, he stuck out his hand as if they were two professionals being introduced at a meeting. The gun across his lap mocked the pleasant expression on his face. "Miss Cotton, it's a pleasure to meet you at last. Tate Cordell."

Tate Cordell? No. Way. "This isn't happening," she muttered. This man couldn't be Tate. "I don't believe you."

"Believe it. I didn't expect to meet you here. Not like this. But our Wyatt is full of surprises." Her stomach curdled at the admiration in his tone. "That was a brilliant move."

"Absolutely the last brilliant thing you'll do," she vowed under her breath. She was getting out of here, even if it meant hiking back to the casino in her heels. Frostbite was better than whatever they had planned.

Wedged between Wyatt and the other man in the back seat, she leaned forward and batted aside the boss's outstretched hand. "You can't be Tate Cordell. The real Tate emailed me this morning. He's a reputable investor currently waiting out the storm in Rapid City."

The man slapped the driver in the shoulder. "See, Baker, I told you it was believable."

"Guess I owe you twenty bucks." Baker glanced at her in the rearview mirror, an unsavory glint in his gaze.

"But you sent the money."

"You make an affordable patsy," Tate said, as if ten grand was petty cash. "We gave ourselves a tour of your staging barn. Looks good. And your business proposal is sound. If I were legit it would've been a smart investment. Go ahead and keep the money. For the assist out of the casino and the general inconvenience."

Rattled, it took her several seconds to process his words. One of these men broke into the barn last night. This morning she'd had hope. Now she was a hostage, surrounded by criminals, and if she survived this, her business might be lost anyway. She couldn't build up a legitimate business on a foundation of criminal funding.

She lunged at Tate, ready to claw the smirk right off his face. The stranger to her left hauled her back. "Get your hands off me!" Before she realized his intention, he'd looped a plastic tie around her wrists and zipped it tight.

"Is that necessary, Karl?" Wyatt asked. "Where can she go?" He wriggled around, buckling the seatbelt under her hands and over her lap.

"Gee, thanks. Now you're thinking of my safety?"

"Always."

She glared at him, refusing to dignify that outrageous lie with any kind of response. Unable to bear looking at him, she deliberately turned her gaze to the windshield. How many mistakes could one woman make? She'd trusted Wyatt when they were kids and he'd crushed her. Yes, she'd vetted Tate

Cordell as an investor and clearly been fooled by the details available online.

The back end of the SUV shimmied as Baker took a turn too fast through the wet, compacted snow. "Do you even know how to drive in these conditions?"

"He's fine," Tate barked.

"At this rate, your driver will kill us before you can spend the cash you stole."

"You think I showed up for a little petty theft?" He snorted. "We just stole a fortune in diamonds, including the Mae West Solitaire."

Baker and Karl gave a cheer, but she noticed Wyatt's reticence. It was hardly enough to explain or excuse his involvement here. According to the press during that era Mae West claimed the diamond was too big to wear often and too small to be cursed. At the moment, it felt pretty cursed to Evie.

"Karl come on with the gear." Tate snapped his fingers. "I'm cold."

The tires fishtailed again. The smart move was to hunker down and wait out this storm. Well, the smartest move was not to rob a casino in the first place. But since they had, they should be going south toward potentially clear roads. Baker, presumably obeying Tate's orders, seemed determined to be winding his way north.

"Why did you take me?" she asked Wyatt.

"That's enough out of you." Tate bounced into the door as Baker skidded around a downed tree limb. "Keep her quiet," he snarled at Wyatt.

While Karl was doubled over the rear seat for the stash of coats and cold-weather gear, she used the distraction and the swaying vehicle, trying to unbuckle her seatbelt with her cuffed hands.

Wyatt caught her. "Stop it, right now." He pressed his elbow into her belly to hold her still. His blue gaze bored straight through her with laser-like intensity. Not unlike the time she'd sliced open her arm after taking a tumble on a trail. Then it had been comforting as he cleaned the wound for her. Right now, she had no idea how to reconcile that potent look with his criminal actions.

She sucked in a sharp breath when he released her. "You won't get away with this," she vowed. She tried to kick his shins just on principle, but he caught her wrists in his hands and gripped hard. Under his grasp, the cuffs dug into her cold skin. She gasped, hating the sheen of tears that blurred her vision.

"Behave," he said the word soundlessly.

It hurt more than her pride that she was caught here. She had to find a way out before they were so far out of town that she'd die of exposure if she escaped. From her vantage point, she scanned the dashboard, wincing when she saw the outside temperature was reading ten degrees below zero. Add in the wind and her odds of surviving anything more than a short walk were slim to none. She knuckled away a tear from her cheek before the men noticed.

Tate, Karl, and Wyatt were wrestling themselves into coats, gloves and scarves, stomping into boots. More confirmation of Wyatt's willing choice to be here.

"Got anything in my size?" she asked Karl, just in case.

"Let him keep you warm," Karl said, aiming a sly look over her head to Wyatt.

Repulsed, she shrank back into her seat. She wasn't getting out, not yet anyway, but she couldn't give up. She pressed her hands between her thighs, hoping her temper would keep her warm.

Wyatt grumbled. "Come on, man. Do we have anything to keep her warm?" Without waiting for Karl to move, he unbuckled and twisted around to look for himself. Righting himself, he dragged a blanket over her lap and pulled it up, tucking it around her shoulders.

"Thanks." It was hard to even give him that much. It was probably smart that her hands were tied. She wanted to strangle him. She pressed her lips together to keep her teeth from chattering. The reaction was more about the nerves at this point than the cold.

Under the blanket, she cautiously stretched her wrists against the zip tie. Did Wyatt realize he'd given her a chance to escape? Of everyone in this car, he should know she wouldn't give up.

Sure she was only one woman against three armed men in the middle of the worst blizzard in nearly a century. There were better odds at a roulette table.

No matter, Evie had been making her own luck for years now.

"Can't you go faster?" Tate asked Baker.

He pressed on the accelerator and the wheels spun. "Not if I don't have to."

"Are there chains on the tires?" she asked Wyatt. He shook his head. "Then turn south."

He pressed a finger to his lips, the universal signal for silence.

"Keep her quiet," Tate warned. "Karl, anything on the police scanner?"

Evie turned to the man on her left. She hadn't even noticed Karl working with a handheld scanner. "Nothing. I don't know if the network is down or if they just aren't moving."

"Both, most likely," Wyatt said, echoing Evie's thoughts.

"They don't believe you'll get far," she said. "I'd have to agree," she added. Baker wasn't giving her much confidence that he could handle this oversized vehicle in the deepening snow. "You realize you're only a few blocks from the casino."

She suspected the snow was muddling Baker's sense of direction, though there weren't a great many ways to get lost once you were on the main highway.

"Quiet," Wyatt pleaded.

"Let me out and I won't be your problem anymore," she snapped.

"We should let her go," Baker said. He glanced in the rearview mirror. "We dump her and keep going. Gives us a little space, especially if anyone follows us."

"Just keep driving," Tate said. "We might need her later. If something happens to Wyatt, she can take over as our guide."

She glared at her old friend. "I hate you." It was predictable and lame. It was so very high school, but it was the worst thing she could think of right now.

"I know," he replied.

"I'll never forgive you for this," she added after another few minutes.

"I know."

Was that all he had? "You were smart once. This... this is an unbelievable low. Even for you."

He faced her down. "What does that mean?"

"You *know*." She tried to avoid slamming into Wyatt as Baker momentarily lost control of the SUV again. There were videos online about how to escape zip ties. Why had she never watched them? "If you're the guide, guide him to a safer route."

Tate swiveled in his seat. "She knows where we're going?"

"Of course not," Wyatt said. "She isn't supposed to be here at all."

She didn't look away in time and the mean flare in Tate's gaze made her shiver. He reached over and turned up the heat, aiming a vent right at her.

"Better?"

"Yes, thank you." Better to agree with whatever he said at

this point. When she'd seen pictures of Tate online, he'd seemed a polite professional. Of course now she knew it had all been a setup. In person, the hard edges were evident, along with a dark intent that frankly unnerved her.

Questions pelted her from all sides, most of them about how Wyatt had ever gotten tangled up with Tate. She didn't dare ask those. Instead, she wondered why the man had targeted her. It was silly to give in to her hurt feelings when she might be killed at any moment, on purpose or by Baker's inexperience behind the wheel.

"Why even pretend you were interested in my business?"

"I wanted a tour of the area," Tate admitted. "Your company was the best fit for me."

"Why?"

"What are you doing?" Wyatt asked in a hiss.

"Trying to understand how any of this happened." She leaned forward, heedless that the blanket slipped forward. "Why, Mr. Cordell?" she repeated.

"Cottonwood is a small company," Tate answered. "A small company in some financial stress worked to my advantage, plus with off-season I was guaranteed the best possible local guide. You."

She sat back again and resumed her efforts to break free of the zip tie under the blanket.

"Don't pout, Evelyn," Tate said. "When I contacted you, my hope was to get enough information from you so your old pal there couldn't screw me over. He tells me we'll have a tough time reaching the rendezvous point in this weather. I'm tempted to ask if you agree."

She didn't want to know where the rendezvous point was. If he told her, an escape would be even more difficult. "We'll have a tough time going another mile," Evie muttered.

"He warned me it would be easier to hike part of it."

She nearly choked. It was all she could do to keep the reaction off her face and keep her gaze away from Wyatt. They were driving north to a destination easier to reach on foot. Tate probably thought he was being vague, but Evie knew Wyatt too well. And like Wyatt, she knew the area too well.

They must be headed toward the ghost town that had once been a thriving community during the Black Hills gold rush. If she could get away, and reach the police before she froze in the weather, the authorities might catch them in time.

Beside her, Wyatt was stiff, a muscle in his jaw jumping, a sure sign of his frustration and stress. It shouldn't have been any comfort at all and yet... it was a sign she recognized from long ago. That muscle would react whenever his mother embarrassed him or when he had to go smooth over her debts or insult with someone in town.

If he was stressed about this, maybe he wasn't here because he wanted to be. The outrageous thought stuck in her head, refused to budge. Did she have an ally in this car? She bumped his knee with her own.

"Let me go," she said. "I don't care what you stole or where you're going." Baker took a curve too quickly and Karl fell into her, pressing her up against Wyatt. "He's going to get all of us killed."

"Someone shut her up," Tate ordered.

As Baker straightened out the car, taking the majority of the narrow strip the plows had cleared, Karl pulled his scarf from around his neck and started to loop it over her head. Evie reared back, shoving herself more into Wyatt.

"Hold her still," Karl said.

"Leave her alone," Wyatt argued. He reached behind her and shoved Karl back. "She's scared."

"Scared or not I can take *you*," she snapped.

From the front seat, Tate chuckled. It wasn't a pleasant sound. "A hostage with spunk. I like it."

Wyatt covered her mouth with a gloved hand before she could reply. His blue eyes locked with hers. She recognized his silent plea for her to cooperate. Subsiding, she righted herself as best she could considering Baker's lack of control at the wheel. Her stomach was churning, the bad driving and being a hostage piling up.

She didn't care for Tate's tone or the gleam of interest in his eyes when he looked at her. The man had a mean streak he'd hidden well. She supposed hiding and manipulation were good skills for a thief. That still didn't explain how Wyatt got mixed up in all of this.

Needing that answer, hoping her best friend hadn't slipped beyond redemption, she sat back, deciding to bide her time. In this weather there would be an opening and when it came, she'd be ready to make her move, with luck, Wyatt would escape with her.

CHAPTER SEVEN

SHE HATED HIM. She thought he was a criminal. He struggled to put the pain of that and the rest of his reeling emotions aside. It was too late to change anything for her and dividing his focus could prove disastrous.

Mentally, he blasted Pickering and the FBI order to stand down. He resented that what should be a golden opportunity had devolved into a mess of epic proportions. The shock, disappointment, and anger he'd seen in Evie's expressive gray eyes would haunt him for the rest of his days.

Of course, those days might not add up to much if Baker didn't get control of the vehicle.

All his life, despite the ugly rumors and uglier truth that cycled through town about his mom, Evie had stood by him. Stood up for him. For as long as he could remember, she refused to lump him into the same category as his addicted mother. At every opportunity, she'd spout off about anything good he'd done, from acing a spelling test to helping her rebuild a snowblower.

And how had he repaid her? He'd left without saying goodbye.

She had valid cause to hate him long before he'd returned to Deadwood. Shame coursed through him for hoping he might have gotten in and out of town without seeing her. Although, in light of the situation, it clearly would've been better if he'd never seen her.

So many things could have gone differently, if only he'd trusted her. Then and now.

He sensed the shift in her body. Never one to give up, she was looking for the opening and fighting to break out of the zip ties so she could take it when it came.

"Ease up on this curve, Baker," he said.

The man gripped the wheel harder. "You wanna drive?"

"I will if you can't," Wyatt replied.

"Baker drives." Tate ended the discussion. "You said this road would get us to the spur."

"In clear conditions we'd be halfway to the turn-off by now," Wyatt said. If he knew Evie, she'd figured out Cordell's intended destination, but he wanted to make it clear. "You should've kept the original schedule," he added to get under the man's skin.

Tate twisted in his seat. "If I'd waited, we'd have bad roads and cops on our tail. This is better."

In their initial calls, Cordell had struck Wyatt as an average thief and he wasn't sure why the FBI was so hot to catch him, aside from the embarrassment that he kept escaping with small, prominent fortunes. In person, the well-above-average cunning came through. On the job, the man was intimidating and left no doubt about who was in charge.

And now that he was sitting in the middle of the operation it was easier to understand how and why Cordell's crew evaded the authorities. Cordell might appear to be acting randomly, but he'd thought through and anticipated every detail. He kept loyal men with him and created redundancies that protected them all from the new guy.

Evie was a redundancy Cordell wasn't ready to relinquish. He believed Evie and Wyatt were interchangeable. When it came to local trails, in clear weather, he was mostly right. But if Cordell had relied on coincidence to find a backup for Wyatt, the FBI would've caught him a long time ago. Despite the distraction of nasty weather, the man had to be somewhat suspicious of Wyatt taking this particular woman hostage.

Based on the FBI's background, a suspicious Cordell was a ruthless and dangerous man. With ice gathering on the inside of the windows, his priority shifted to protecting Evie over the FBI's agenda. How was he going to get her out of this safely?

Although Baker was learning how to handle the icy curves, Wyatt couldn't shake the feeling that they were walking a tightrope. He'd been out here in storms only half as bad as Holly and he knew it was a matter of time before the roads became impassable. Plus, he'd hauled Evie out of the casino with no protection against the elements. Her uniform of black slacks, a crisp cotton shirt, the black and silver vest, western bolo tie, and the black heels would be no help when she did try to escape. And she would.

Her best chance was if he could get them to turn back toward town. "It's possible the spur we need hasn't been plowed," he said. "Or even salted." That was assuming they could find the turn-off at all. Visibility was dwindling with every minute.

Cordell shook his head. "You're just now mentioning this?" he asked, his tone rumbling in a low growl. Ruthless. Dangerous.

There was little point arguing, but Wyatt held his ground. "I mentioned it earlier. This morning and yesterday. You said the rendezvous schedule wasn't negotiable."

Evie pressed her lower leg to his. He didn't deserve

anything close to support right this second, but he was damn happy to have it.

"That's why we moved early." Cordell swore. "Figure it out, Jameson. There must be more than one road in this state."

Wyatt stopped Evie before she could say something provoking and tried to make sense of what he could see through the windows. It was all a haze of white, nearly impossible to distinguish the shadows of trees from rocky outcroppings. Cordell had researched the diamonds, the casino, and the people. Why hadn't the man put more effort into researching the terrain?

Because he'd hired Wyatt, an expert on the area who was disenchanted with all things legal after the military cut him loose for getting injured on a patrol. Then he'd tried to use Evie as research but this blasted winter storm interfered.

The SUV slowed as Baker eased off the gas and coasted to a stop. Snow had drifted into a high bank that blocked the road. "What now?" He used the rearview mirror to shoot a dark look at Wyatt.

"Remind me never to doubt the weather girl again," Evie said. "At least she still has her job. Thanks to you, I'm sure my career at the Silver Aces is over."

"Better a job than your life," Wyatt said. Dealing poker wasn't a career for Evie anyway, but this was hardly the time to point that out.

"Guess you'll have to turn back," Evie quipped. Her false cheer filled the vehicle and Wyatt knew he was the only one amused. "Can you manage a three-point turn or do I need to handle it?" she asked sweetly.

Wyatt bumped her knee. "Knock it off." He appreciated her attempt to be annoying enough that Cordell would toss her out, but it wasn't in her best interest. They were too far from any shelter for her to survive the storm. He had to come up with something and fast.

"Miss Cotton, listen to your pal and shut up," Cordell agreed. "I'm waiting for a solution, Jameson."

She fixed her gaze on the windshield and wisely kept quiet. He did the same, watching the wipers slap uselessly against the heavy snowstorm. "Either we get out and hike from here or we back it up and take the next available road," Wyatt said with a sigh. "In my opinion, we're better off going back. A longer drive, but less risk of exposure in this weather."

Cordell turned to Evie. "You agree with him?"

"I don't know where you're going," she said. "Though the clearest route out of the storm is to the south."

Cordell scowled. "Of course you'd want us to go back through town."

Evie shrugged and Wyatt drew the thief's attention. "Clear is relative," he said. "This storm is massive." But if they were closer to town, he could get her out of the car before guiding Cordell and his men the long way around to the ghost town. The GPS tracker in his wallet was built to hold up so the FBI could pick up their quarry. Every hour he could keep them in transition gave Evie a better chance to notify the authorities of their destination.

"Do it," Cordell said to Baker. "Turn around."

Baker's hesitation was almost imperceptible, but it was something. Wyatt filed the reaction away. If he could get the others to turn on Cordell, their chances of survival increased. Slowly, with extreme caution Baker backed up until he had the space to turn the car around.

"Excellent," Evie declared. "You'll get caught and I can clear my name. Hundreds of cameras cover the highway in Deadwood. No industry has more watchdog tendencies than the casinos."

He recognized her ramping up into a tirade and let her ramble, just to see Cordell's reaction.

"The law around here doesn't cater to thieves and kidnappers," she continued. "Even if you get away today, Sheriff Russell will track you down. You should—"

He shoved his elbow into her ribs. "That's enough, Evelyn." He said her name with a sneer that he knew would get under her skin. One of the perks of knowing another person so well.

She gawked at him. "You're the worst."

He wished he could assure her he wasn't. It was just more motivation to get both of them out of this in one piece so he could explain everything and prove he hadn't given up on being an honorable man.

"I'm not going to post bail or visit you in prison," she said, nose in the air.

"Shut up!" Cordell roared. "Or I'll just shoot you and dump you in the snow for a bear."

"The bears are hibernating," she said. The woman never knew when to quit.

Cordell aimed a small revolver at her. Wyatt hadn't known he was carrying that one in addition to the bigger, semi-automatic he'd used in the robbery. At this range the revolver could be deadly enough. Beside him Evie paled. "Easy," Wyatt said. "She's a complication we can turn to our advantage, especially in town."

"We'll see." Cordell lowered the gun.

Evie didn't look all that grateful. Wyatt knew she was fuming and plotting her way out of the vehicle. He didn't blame her. In her place, he'd do the same thing. He just hoped she had the patience to let him assist.

"If we end up going all the way through town having her along forces the cops to think twice before taking aggressive measures," he said, outlining the main reason they should keep Evie with them. "Not to mention if something happens to me, you have your backup expert."

It wasn't the smartest move to remind Cordell he was expendable, but worth it if it kept Evie alive. She was absolutely right about the cameras, although the lousy visibility played into Cordell's favor. She was also spot on with her theory that the local authorities were waiting for them to kill themselves out here. The robbery was less than an hour old, but it was a safe bet the casino security and the sheriff's office had already broadcast the make, model, and plate number for the SUV over every emergency channel.

On top of that, Agent Pickering and her team were surely following the GPS tracker in his wallet. They were likely the only vehicle on the road in Deadwood right now, so there would be no mistaking them, no place to hide.

Up front, Baker fiddled with the defrost setting to no avail. He leaned forward in the seat, both hands on the wheel again, struggling to pick out the best part of the road in a landscape that was a blur of white on white. The acceleration was subtle. Between the adrenaline and the slippery road Baker probably didn't know his foot was heavy on the gas pedal.

Cordell braced a hand on the dash.

"Ease up, Baker," Wyatt said. "No one's expecting us to come back." It wasn't a lie. Regardless of the FBI tracker, this move wouldn't be expected. "No need to rush."

"I'm not rushing," Baker retorted. "I'm braking."

"Don't," Wyatt and Evie said in unison.

"Just coast," Wyatt advised. Under the blanket, he saw Evie's hands working at the plastic cuffs again. She must be as worried as he was about Baker's inexperience out here.

But Baker noticed the shape of the road too late.

The back end of the SUV fishtailed, the arc swinging wider on the slippery road as Baker overcompensated. Wyatt clamped his lips together, keeping any advice to himself. It wouldn't help. He could see from the set of Baker's jaw the man was beyond hearing anything. His jaw was locked and he was starting to panic.

They slid and skidded past the row of casinos and hotels. Wyatt took comfort in knowing where he was and a distinct lack of police pursuit. No comfort at all in the way the tires lost grip, gliding over the black ice that formed after the snow had been cleared.

Evie pressed close to his side. She'd seen it too, understood what it meant when a road appeared wet. They were in a dangerous situation and approaching a bridge that was notorious for icing over in much milder conditions.

She opened her mouth to warn Baker and Wyatt elbowed her into silence again. She kicked him, though it barely registered through the snow boots. If the crew self-destructed, they had a better chance of getting away. He'd only have to get the tracker into a pocket of one of the three thieves and the FBI would be able to drop a net over Cordell.

"He'll get us killed," she whispered for his ears alone.

Wyatt pressed his leg close, doing what he could to reassure her. He thought about the roadway, the SUV's safety features and said a prayer it would be enough if Baker lost control. Somehow they'd survive. Had to. He couldn't imagine a world without Evie in it, even if she hated him.

The passenger side tires dragged along the plowed and drifted snow just ahead of the bridge. At the sound, Baker's hands jerked on the wheel. The back end slowly swung toward the middle of the roadway.

Wyatt couldn't tear his gaze away from the horror show playing out in front of them as the heavy snowfall piled up on the windshield, the wind sculpting drifts that completely blotted out the bridge marker on either side of the roadway.

A pristine white blanket covered the guard rail, and a thick layer of ice glazed the sign.

None of that registered for Baker. He didn't know the area and he was too consumed with getting his boss out of Deadwood. Wyatt and Evie were pressed into Karl as Baker fought physics in a futile attempt to straighten the wheels and thread the big SUV through the narrowly plowed path.

In a blink, the SUV was sliding sideways across the bridge, gaining speed on the slight decline. The slide quickly morphed into a sickening spin. Cordell shouted and reached for the wheel. Baker pumped the brakes to no avail. The other men shouted as if words would change anything. If Evie made a sound, he couldn't hear it over the others. It was impossible to focus on any one point, the world was a swirl of white through every window.

A piece of the front fender caught on the guard rail and halted the spin with a lurch and an ear-piercing shriek of metal on metal. Wyatt took a breath when the sound stopped, sure it was over, grateful they were safe. But the SUV's momentum carried them on. Baker swore, slamming his hands against the steering wheel as they continued to slide backward down the sloping road.

Wyatt swore and fought to release his seatbelt. He hauled himself into the gap between the front seats, over the console, inadvertently kicking Evie in the shins as he reached for the wheel. Bruises were better than what he feared was coming.

"What are you doing?" Cordell shouted, grabbing his arm.

Wyatt shrugged him off. "Saving your life," he said. He hoped he was saving them all. Catching the steering wheel around Baker's hands, he turned it hard, cranking the tires away from the edge of the roadway that fell away into a ravine. With the storm blowing snow and altering the view, only a local would know the hazard was there.

At last the heavy vehicle stopped moving, the back end tucked into a drift. Not ideal, but enough. For several heartbeats, the only sound was their ragged breathing. In the tense silence, the wind gusted and snow kicked up against the windows. It was like being wrapped in a blanket, except the sense of security was a lie.

"Don't move," Wyatt whispered. He had yet to shift from his position wedged between the front seats. Craning his neck in an awkward angle, his gaze caught Evie's. The concern he saw in her wide, beautiful eyes startled him.

"Get us out of here," Tate barked. "We're sitting ducks."

"No one else is out here," Wyatt reminded him. No one would find them in this weather without the GPS tracker. Even with the device, the risk to the pursuing officers would be considered too high. It was the worst time to think the FBI might have been smart by insisting Pickering's team stay put until the storm passed.

"Whatever." He rubbed his chest. "We've wasted enough time up and down this road. Diamonds or not, I'm starting to hate this town."

"Feel free to leave. Without me," Evie said.

He shot her a look at the quiver in her voice. She was ready to bolt. He couldn't blame her for wanting out of the car, but he was relieved that she wasn't moving. So she, like him, realized disaster hovered too close for comfort.

"Are we on the road?"

"I don't know," he admitted.

"What's that mean?" Karl asked, panicking.

"Well, hell, we just have to find out," Cordell complained, pushing open his door.

"Wait!" Wyatt cried, but it was too late. The SUV shifted sideways. The door fell back into place and the cold metal frame creaked as the SUV dropped.

Baker stomped on the brake pedal, a useless reflex. There

was no chance of regaining control now. Wyatt saw Evie's eyes go round. He tried to use his body as a counterbalance and keep them on the road. A blast of wind howled and he heard a tree snap somewhere close. Fate or gravity did the rest.

"I'm sorry Evie," he said as the SUV fell off the road and down into the ravine.

Her scream echoed forever, punctuated by the sounds of crumpling metal, breaking trees and snow billowing all around them.

All of the words Wyatt needed to say were lodged in his throat. He was stuck in his own personal horror movie, starring as both the monster and the inept boyfriend trying—and failing—to save the girl. She wouldn't be here right now if it wasn't for his rash choice to drag her along when the robbery fell apart. His fault. Her blood on his hands, if she died here, believing he was a criminal. She'd never know how much he still loved her.

He was weightless while the SUV kept falling, Tate and his men alternately yelled prayers and curses while Evie's accusing gaze stayed locked on him. Guilt was his brutal companion and he deserved every injury or consequence for being so careless with her. With his feelings for her.

During his Army days, he'd been in tough situations, but they never went on a mission without a plan. Never without a team he could trust at his side, at his back. Having men and women he could count on, people who didn't care where he'd come from, had been the greatest unexpected benefit of his military career.

Every moment flashed through his mind with frightening clarity. The good and the bad. In Deadwood, on Army bases around the world. What he'd loved. What he'd lost by leaving. He'd been so sure the gains and independence would offset not having Evie in his life. It sucked to know death was imminent and have so many regrets about decisions he couldn't change.

The back end of the SUV crashed through the trees, the rear window shattering. Cold air, broken glass, branches and snow drifted up into the cabin as they continued to fall. Evie was buckled in, but the blanket had fallen away and he could see her hands were still restrained. She seemed to be reaching for him, her hair drifting around her face. Instinctively, he reached for her too, but it was pointless as the crash tossed him around.

The final impact was bone-jarring as the SUV landed on the rear bumper. Wyatt lost his breath, tossed into the side of the passenger seat and pinned when the backseat rushed up to meet him. Those weren't stars dancing in front of his eyes, but dust and debris floating through the air, all of it laced with freezing air and snow. Behind him Cordell groaned and wheezed. He could see blood trickling down Baker's forehead where the driver had collided with the steering wheel.

"Evie?" He tried to twist where he could see her, but he was stuck.

"I'm here." She coughed. "Hold still, hold still."

He relaxed just knowing she was alive. Slowly, his body came out of the initial shock, a wealth of discomforts from head to toe accented by a few clear points of sharp pain. "I'm not hurt," he said.

"Then why are you bleeding?" She'd freed herself from the seatbelt and was dabbing at his cheek with her bound hands. "Can you move?" she asked.

He tried to say yes, but his ribs protested his attempt to breathe. He gave her a thumb's up sign. "Need a minute," he wheezed. He picked up on the coppery scent of blood in the air. They were probably all bleeding in various degrees. Pain pulsed through him in deep, aching waves, but he didn't think he was seriously injured.

The same couldn't be said for the man on the other side of Evie. As Wyatt's vision cleared, he could see that Karl was unconscious at best. Blood pooled behind his head, soaking into the upholstery behind him.

"Take my hands," Evie said. "You can get out this way through the back door."

Urgency filled her voice and he understood her intent. If only it was possible for them to get enough distance to make a run for it. They weren't far from town, assuming they could survive long enough to find a trail out of the ravine, but Cordell was stirring in the passenger seat.

"What now, Jameson?" Cordell asked, his voice strained.

"We get out and find shelter until we can start working our way to the rendezvous," Wyatt answered through gritted teeth. It would be long miles on foot in a raging blizzard with three inexperienced and possibly injured people. "You still have the diamonds?" he asked, knowing the answer.

Cordell patted the pocket under his heavy coat. "Yes," he said, somewhat relieved. "Karl has the solitaire. Karl?"

"Karl's injured," Wyatt said. "He can't move. Evie, you'll need to adjust as Tate gets out so we stay balanced."

"Got it." Her gaze was locked on him.

He'd been away from Evie so long he'd forgotten how nice it was to work this kind of emergency with an expert. "Tate, open your door, slow and steady."

"What's wrong with Karl?" he asked instead.

Wyatt bit back an oath, more than ready to stand up straight again. "When the rest of us are clear, we'll find out." He wondered if anyone actually packed the first aid kit he'd requested. Not that he expected a few bandages would be enough for Karl.

As Cordell climbed out of the SUV, Evie shadowed him so perfectly the vehicle barely moved. "Karl is dead," she whispered so only Wyatt heard.

He gave her an equally imperceptible nod.

One by one, they climbed out of the car, Baker next, then Evie and finally Wyatt. He dropped into the deep snow and verified he had his wallet and the GPS tracker. Following Cordell's footsteps through the snow around to the driver's side, he noticed the vehicle looked worse from the outside than it had felt on the inside.

Baker and Cordell were wrestling with the rear door, unable to pull it open and pull Karl free.

"He's dead." Baker turned his back on the wreck on an oath and kept on swearing. "He's dead!"

Wyatt wasn't in the mood to offer any comfort. Evie was shivering, the blanket doing nothing to protect her feet and legs from the snow. "Someone cut her hands free," he said.

"You don't give the orders," Cordell barked.

"You'll listen if you want to survive," Wyatt barked back. Ignoring the others, he slogged through the snow and kicked out the rear passenger window so he could salvage Karl's gear for Evie and search for anything useful.

"What are you doing?" Evie asked, Cordell right behind her with the same question.

"Karl doesn't need his coat anymore." He passed it to Evie, pleased to see she wasn't cuffed anymore. "Or his boots." He handed those back as well. He searched for a first aid kit and couldn't find one.

"Stop!" Baker shouted. "You can't do this." He tried to take the coat from Evie, but she dodged him.

"I have to." Wyatt had no desire to fight with Baker. The man was strong and in a rage. He side-stepped and ducked under the first swing. "Call him off, Cordell." He ducked again. "You need me. If she gets hurt, I'm out."

Tate raised his revolver, cocked the hammer. The other gun was somewhere in the depths of the wreckage. "You'll cooperate, regardless."

Casually, Wyatt picked up a handful of snow and pressed it to his cheek, washing away the blood. He must have been bitten by flying glass. "Let her wait here," he said. "We don't need her anymore. She'll only slow us down. We have a rendezvous to make."

Between the storm and the crash, making it to the ghost town on time was unlikely. According to the plan, the meet wouldn't have gone Cordell's way anyway. Not with Wyatt working against him so the FBI could gather up the thieves in one tidy net. Of course, the FBI plan was shot too, thanks to the storm.

He had absolutely no idea how he was going to get Cordell, Baker, and the diamonds into FBI custody while giving Evie what she needed to survive.

"One step at a time," Evie murmured from behind him, zipping into Karl's coat.

It was a strange comfort that she could read him so well after all this time. Strange too that she didn't seem quite so angry at him. Maybe it was the shock of the crash. In the big man's coat, she looked small and far too fragile to leave her here alone. He looked up at the road and the long scar the SUV had carved through the trees and snow. If anyone could get up there and find help, it was her.

Cordell wagged his gun between them and Wyatt stepped closer, blocking his angle on Evie. "Let's get moving," Wyatt said.

He hated leaving Evie here. The outer gear and a crumpled SUV wouldn't be enough protection from the elements. The heavy snow was piling up too fast. At this rate it would take days for Deadwood to dig out and get back to normal, much less find the signs an SUV had gone over the edge of the road.

"Fine." Cordell lowered the revolver and stuffed it into a

pocket. He moved before Wyatt could stop him and grabbed the coat. "Give me the Mae West."

Without a word, she pulled out a small velvet bag and handed it over.

"Lead the way," Cordell said. "I'm not missing my ride out of this hellhole."

Wyatt bit his tongue. Cordell didn't want to miss the payday he'd lined up for the diamonds.

"Be smart," Evie said, using the phrase her father taught them.

Dale Cotton had always said the best tool in any crisis was a clear mind. Whether they'd been leading a tubing group or hiking up to one of the mines, it was imperative not to take even familiar terrain for granted. Today was a prime example that Mother Nature had her own agenda.

"You too," he replied under his breath. It was as much assurance as he could give her right now. He paused, searching her somber gray eyes. Was it only his wishful thinking, or did she realize he would come back for her?

Feeling like a jerk, he led Cordell and Baker away from the crash site. Wyatt had to trust her to survive so he could explain himself one day. He couldn't give up on her stubbornness, her sheer willpower, or her grit. He'd need to pull those same qualities out of himself.

The two men behind him didn't speak, though they were far from silent. They trudged through the blowing storm with grunts of effort and boots stomping and shuffling through the deep snow. Wyatt intended to wear them out by nightfall, leading them well off the track from the intended rendezvous.

Just as soon as he figured out where to park them while he waited for the FBI pick-up.

CHAPTER EIGHT

USING THE SUV AS A WINDBREAK, Evie watched Wyatt leave. Within minutes, all three men were lost in the swirling white of the storm. She burrowed into the coat, ignoring the stain of Karl's blood near the collar, while she debated her options. First, she had to survive. Shoving her feet into the boots, she cinched the ties as snug as they would go. They were still too big, but they should stay on when she moved. And she would move. She couldn't ride out the storm here.

Her cheeks stung and she sipped the frigid air through cupped hands. Inching back to the dead man, she decided the blood-stained scarf wasn't an option. Closing his eyes, she took Karl's gloves and then looked around for anything else that might be useful.

She was sad a life had been lost, even a thief's life, but this wasn't the time or place to be finicky about resources. Finding a knife in the side pocket of his pants, she slipped it into the inside pocket of the coat and kept searching. To her shock, one pocket was full of loose diamonds.

"Were you trying to cheat Cordell?" She tucked the stones

into her coat and zipped the pocket closed. "That wouldn't have ended well for you even if you'd lived."

A gust of wind pushed snow into her face and she retreated to a more protected part of the totaled SUV. Her neck was sore, her shoulders too. Hunkering down, keeping still would make all of that worse. She'd have bruises from shoulder to thigh. Assuming she lived long enough for them to form.

What did it mean that Wyatt not only remembered her dad's advice, but gave her the words? He'd chosen a fine time to channel her dad, to remind her of better days when they'd been friends and Wyatt her most trusted ally.

She couldn't dwell on what was. He was working with a criminal and he'd left her here to fend for herself. The smart move was finding shelter. Squinting up at the slope she discarded the idea of climbing back up to the road. The direct path was not the best route in this case.

Even if she had the gear to climb back up to the road, it wasn't as if she could count on help from a passing driver. Everyone with sense was hunkered down and waiting out the storm. Tate's worries about being chased had been completely unfounded. The sheriff was too smart to put his deputies in danger on these roads. Probably the only thing that had worked in his favor during the robbery.

And none of that got her out of here. She could follow Wyatt with relative ease and interfere with their getaway. They were headed north to Garden City, the famous mining ghost town. Not that it made any sense to stick with that plan in this weather.

Be smart, she repeated to herself. She'd always found it baffling the way her father trusted her to be smart in the field and not in the business office. On a groan, she stamped her feet in the boots to give her feet a jolt. Maybe she should take Karl's pants too. The thought made her cringe, but her thin uniform pants were no match for this weather.

When she was bundled up again, the hood covering as much of her face as possible, she forced herself to be logical. Leaving the SUV meant wandering through a blizzard that blurred the landmarks. Getting turned around was a real danger.

She briefly considered setting the SUV on fire. It would be a ginormous equivalent of a flare, but again, no one else was out here to see it. Watching the wind shape the snow into drifts around the wrecked vehicle, she knew she had to leave. If she tried to use the SUV for shelter, she'd be swallowed by the storm within a few hours. No one would find her until the spring thaw.

She thought of Wyatt insisting she take Karl's gear. The way he stepped in front of that revolver. Remembered the intensity in his gaze as they fell off the road. And his apology, the words she wasn't even sure she'd heard, echoed in her mind.

He was sorry. For leaving her in Deadwood eleven years ago, or coming back just to leave her again—in the worst snowstorm in a century? It didn't matter at this point. There was more to this situation, more to *him*, than what she could see on the surface. However he was tied to Tate Cordell, she didn't believe it was simple.

Wyatt was not a criminal. As much as she wanted to cling to that excuse to hate him, she had other reasons. And every last one of them felt petty and small right now.

Which meant she couldn't leave him out in this mess alone with armed men determined to get away with a serious crime. She started to trudge after them, keeping her steps in line with theirs, though Holly was doing her best to erase the trail.

There were a few tourism properties and hunting cabins

on this side of the road that could be used for shelter. The closest one she could think of was an abandoned miner's cabin. Could Wyatt plan to wait out the storm there? If she was going to help him, she had to remember his habits, choices and strengths.

At one time, they'd been the closest of friends. Inseparable. Able to anticipate thoughts and decisions, practically finishing each other's sentences. She'd helped him wallow or ignore his mother's antics as her gambling addiction demolished everything around him. He'd helped her dream up ways to build an adventuring business, the only thing she'd ever wanted to do.

How much of her predicament was her fault? She'd told him she wanted him to do whatever he was here to do. He'd asked her to ride out the storm at home. Looked like she was the one breaking promises this time.

As epiphanies went, it would've been more comfortable having this one around a roaring fire with thick socks on her feet and her hands wrapped around a steaming mug of hot chocolate.

She kept moving forward while her mind wandered. She pushed aside thoughts of the past. Old pain and anger weren't the way to focus. Instead, she imagined Tate and Baker in handcuffs. Not that she had any. She was a poker-dealing adventure guide, not law enforcement. And she'd be neither if this storm had its way.

She added Sheriff Russell to her fantasy, heard his mellow voice reading the men their rights before commending Wyatt for his brave undercover work. Yeah, that was a much better scenario than thinking of him as a criminal.

Within minutes, both layers of pants were soaked through and the cold, wet fabric sapped her body heat. Resting one hand on the nearest tree for balance, she glanced back over her shoulder. Blowing snow was all she could see in any direction. She used the tree to pull herself forward. One step at a time. The bitter cold and low visibility couldn't matter.

She would outsmart this storm and help Wyatt survive. That was the only way to get the answers and explanations she'd wanted for eleven years.

USING THE RIDGE AS A GUIDE, Wyatt continued moving to the north as fast as he could manage. His leg raged at him, protesting with every step. He resented every polar-fleece, sub-zero outerwear manufacturer that made life easier on Cordell and Baker. The men weren't quitting. They were barely slowing him down. Maybe he'd underestimated the incentive of millions of dollars in diamonds.

It sure wasn't an easy way to make money.

If he couldn't lose the men and circle back to Evie soon, she'd be in big trouble. That was not an acceptable outcome. The constant howl of the wind made normal conversation impossible, a definite bonus considering the way Cordell's voice grated on his nerves. Cell phones were useless and Cordell believed a radio would reveal their position to the police.

And the snow just kept piling up.

Other than the occasional stumble, neither of the men showed any sign of giving in. Great. At this point he didn't care if the diamonds were lost or if the FBI put him out of business for not delivering the robbery crew as promised.

As if he had any say in the weather or a madman who'd exposed them to this extreme danger. He leaned into another surge of snow and wind. When the gust was done, he glanced back, seeing Cordell and Baker huddled together.

Plotting his demise probably. Fools. They'd never get out

of here without a guide in this weather. "Let's go!" he shouted just to see what they'd do.

Both men were impossible to read through the layers of outerwear, but Wyatt was sure the gun was in Cordell's hand. Whether or not he could fire it accurately was the question.

"We need shelter," Cordell shouted, loping awkwardly toward him.

Evie needed shelter, Wyatt thought darkly. These two needed a jail cell. "That's the plan," he hollered back.

"Baker was hurt in the crash." Cordell said. "He can't go much longer."

It was the first good news Wyatt had heard in hours. Days, really. "How bad?" he asked, moving back through his tracks to where Baker was propped against a tree.

"Ribs maybe? I'm no doctor," Cordell said. "Do something. He's breathing weird."

They were all breathing weird in this nasty wind and snow. Under the scarf Baker was pale. His breathing was shallow and jerky. Pained. Definitely ribs. "Can't help him out here," Wyatt said. He didn't bother mentioning the many rugged miles between them and the rendezvous.

"Obviously," Cordell snarled. "Give me solutions."

Wyatt mentally cussed out Cordell, the weather-phobic FBI, his gambling-addict mother and the world at large for bringing him to this moment of pure insanity. They had yet to find an abandoned mine shaft.

Yes, he believed in taking ownership of decisions and choices. Yes, he'd left Deadwood to make something of himself in the military. And he had, only to trash it all by returning to town with a band of thieves.

He cringed, thinking of how the robbery must look to the Silver Aces security team. The many surveillance camera angles would show the hometown military hero kidnap Evie while helping the crew escape.

If the FBI didn't clear that up with a very public statement, he was screwed, his new career up in smoke. Or buried in snow. Either way it was over. Evie had to survive. Had to. His soul would shatter if she didn't. Of course if she survived he had no doubt she'd gleefully testify against him if there was a trial.

He caught the tail of his scattering thoughts. This must be his brain with frostbite. "The only chance he has is to keep going. There's a mining museum up ahead, and we might find a hunting cabin before that."

Cordell didn't look pleased, but unless he wanted to build an igloo or had a pop-up tent in his pocket, the only choice was to press on.

A wild screech sliced through the air before a gust caught the sound and carried it away. It sounded remarkably like Evie's screech owl impersonation. She'd mastered it to amuse young campers and impress skeptical adults on various summer tours.

Fantastic. Now he was hearing things. There was no chance any animal, especially not a small bird, was out in this weather. Finding shelter became more important, regardless of whether or not it helped Baker.

Two short screeches sounded again as he guided them north, Baker supported between them.

"What is that?" Cordell asked.

"Nature," Wyatt replied. That was definitely Evie. He didn't know if he should be relieved or irritated.

The more intriguing question was how she'd gotten so close. When the sound cut through the wind again, he thought she might actually be ahead of them. He kept walking as if it was perfectly normal for an owl to be hunting in the middle of an afternoon blizzard.

"You're lost, aren't you?" Cordell accused as they all paused to catch their breath.

"I'm not." Wyatt pointed toward the wall of snow-covered trees ahead of them. "Can't you see the road?"

Cordell shoved him. "Quit messing with me."

Wyatt, drained mentally and physically, fell into the snow. It was damn tempting to stay put and let the weather have its way. But Evie was close. That was a miracle he couldn't ignore. He hauled himself back to his feet just as Baker groaned and doubled over. "The road is *behind* the trees. Look at the spacing."

Cordell peered ahead, snow coating his eyebrows and eyelashes. "Does that mean we're close?"

Wyatt nodded. "On the other side of this next curve is the road to the mining museum." He didn't tell them it would be at least another mile on that road. We can wait out the weather there." For all the good it would do. They would get snowed in and miss their escape driver waiting at the ghost town.

On top of that, the power would surely be out, and they'd have to break in. Which meant compromising the shelter. But it was better than nothing. If he could keep them there long enough, the FBI could follow the GPS signal and scoop them up the moment the weather cleared.

"Let's move," Baker said, shuffling ahead, carving a path in the wet snow. "I can't feel my face." In a normal storm, that path might've helped the authorities. In this weather, there was no chance the trail would last long enough.

"Me either," Wyatt agreed, taking the easier trail directly in Baker's wake.

The screech sounded, this time much closer. A gunshot followed. He turned in time to see Cordell struggling to pull the trigger again.

Wyatt dropped low and skidded into the man's legs like a big league hitter stealing home. Cordell went down, howling in pain.

Wyatt ran, aiming for the last place he'd heard Evie's screech owl. His legs were heavy, his cold, wet clothing making the task harder still. It felt like running in a nightmare, when every fiber of his being urged him to move faster and his body wouldn't cooperate.

Cordell fired another shot and the bullet bit into a tree to Wyatt's left. He veered away from the shower of snow and bark. Spotting Evie gave him a much needed jolt of adrenaline.

She tugged him down into a hollow created by a fallen tree and the thick blanket of snow. It wasn't exactly a secure hideout since his track through the snow would be obvious for a little while, but he didn't hear anyone shouting or tramping behind him.

"Evie." The break from the blowing wind was almost as wonderful as seeing her. "How did you get ahead of us?" And how much had the weather compromised his judgment if he hadn't noticed her so close?

"You didn't think I'd sit around waiting at the SUV."

"Well, no," he admitted. What would she do if he kissed her? She'd most likely punch him. Regret followed in the wake of relief. After all of this, she might never let him touch her properly again. "I expected you to head back to the casino."

"You're not a criminal."

She'd spoken with such intense bitterness, he laughed. "And that annoys you."

"It does." Abruptly, she pressed a bulky glove-covered hand to his mouth and cocked her head, listening. Her touch, such as it was, sent another jolt through him. He didn't hear anything but wind-driven snow and the creak of tree limbs bending under the heavy weight.

When she scooted back into the shadows of their hideout

he missed that brief contact desperately. "We can't sit here and wait to be shot," he whispered.

"We shouldn't jump out into an ambush either." She pressed her gloved hands to her face. "He isn't built for this weather and he doesn't know his way around the area."

"Cordell's greed and worry over Baker will trump hunting us down."

"Let's hope," she said.

"I thought they'd drop long before now," he said. "Baker's injured. I told them we could shelter at the mining museum."

"Without you they don't stand a chance," she said. "Come over here and we'll stay warm while we wait a bit."

It was the sweetest invitation he'd ever heard. He wedged himself next to her, their combined body heat easing the sting of cold in his fingers and toes. "I'm not a criminal," he blurted. "Never was. I'm working undercover for the FBI."

She wrapped her arms around her knees, her gaze a little sad. "You could've said something."

"No." He shook his head. "I wanted to tell you the second I saw you."

"You could've told me when I stopped by your hotel room," she pointed out.

His lack of trust hurt her feelings. It should've made him sad, instead he was recharged, hopeful that she felt that connection between them coming back to life. "The FBI was listening. Once Cordell reached out to you, they were watching you, too. I couldn't take the chance and blow everything. You told me you'd stay home."

"And if I had you'd be out here alone."

Her eyes flashed and he braced for the punch she would've thrown at his shoulder or his nose if they were younger. He deserved that and much, much more.

"Why?" she asked.

He didn't need her to clarify. "The FBI promised me a

hefty payout if I could lead the crew into their net. I needed the capital and connections to start my own business."

"What business? You should have years left in the army. Is being a trail guide for thieves a viable career?"

He rolled his eyes. Cautiously, he took her hand and pulled off the borrowed glove. Then he placed her hand low on his leg where his calf muscle had once been. "The Army says I'm not good enough to serve anymore."

"Well, they're stupid."

He smiled; his ego puffed up. He could always count on Evie to be on his side. "After burning my bridges here, I started a business as a private investigator out in Sioux Falls."

She sucked in a sharp breath and pressed her lips together, ducking her chin into the collar of her coat. He could only see her eyes and the accusation and hurt was clear even in the shadows, but she didn't release his hand.

"No, I never planned to come back to Deadwood," he said, answering the unspoken question.

"But—"

"We were kids," he said softly. "Worse, I was the kid from *that* family. No one trusted my mom. No one trusted me not to turn into her."

"I did," she insisted. "We were supposed to make something of Cottonwood Adventures."

The sadness in her voice wrecked him. "I know. I'm sorry, Evie." He'd thought leaving had been hard. Sitting here, facing down her lost trust and shattered faith in him was worse. He tucked her hand back into the warm glove. "I thought I was doing the right thing, going out to make something of myself."

To his amazement, she moved closer and rested her head on his shoulder. "I was too hurt, too young to understand that at the time."

"And I was too self-absorbed to consider how my choices

might hurt you." He was afraid to move, afraid that any shift would break the spell and this would all be a strange snow-induced mirage. "Evie, you were indestructible."

"Today would prove I still am."

"True." But it had been a close call and pure terror for him from the robbery to the SUV crashing down the hill. "In my mind, your plans and dreams were a given, with or without me around. What happened?"

"Life lessons. Business lessons." He felt her shrug. "Who knows? Our first hires to replace you were less than ideal and Dad lost patience. Lost interest day by day after mom died. He refuses to expand, insists I go find something meaningful to do with my life."

That surprised him. Dale Cotton had always been a source of common sense and wisdom. Then again, losing Evie would wreck him as losing his wife must have wrecked Dale.

"Cottonwood Adventures is meaningful." He couldn't see her doing anything else. "It's your purpose."

She gave a snort and a puff of vapor clouded between them. "A shame you're the only man in my life who ever noticed that." They cuddled in the quiet, not exactly warm but no longer freezing. The wind eased up and the fat snowflakes were falling straight to the ground rather than blowing horizontally across the opening of their small shelter.

"Cordell isn't this patient," he said after a few more minutes. "He would've followed my trail and barged in leading with bullets by now."

"Then let's move." She sat up and rubbed her hands up and down her thighs.

"Are those Karl's pants?" he asked.

"I don't want to talk about it." She adjusted the collar and hood around her face. "If you sent them to the museum, we can make it to the Greenbriar Goldrush site. It isn't too far. We can wait there for the worst of this to pass."

She started toward the opening and he caught the hem of her coat, stopping her. If he underestimated Cordell, he wouldn't allow her head to be the first one in the line of fire.

She looked over her shoulder, her gray eyes full of questions. Helpless to resist, he tugged her close and kissed her. She didn't fight him off. No, she gripped his coat and pressed her body close to his.

The sudden, sweet-hot contact, the rightness of it burned through the past hurts, cauterizing those old wounds and making room for a spark of something fresh and clean. If only they were anywhere but here, dealing with a blizzard and a diamond thief who wasn't likely to leave loose ends. He eased back, his heart pounding. The aches in his body now had nothing to do with the earlier crash.

He crept to the edge of the shelter and paused to listen before moving through. No bullets, no threatening promises from Cordell.

"We're not done," Evie said from behind him.

He couldn't agree more.

CHAPTER NINE

EVIE WAS PRETTY sure that kiss might be enough to keep her warm through a week of blizzard conditions without proper shelter. Wyatt hadn't lost his touch or his ability to send her system into overdrive. Desire-infused fantasies drifted through her mind, messing with her concentration, each one better than the last.

But the pulsing, rekindled desire had to wait. She needed to focus if they were going to make the Greenbriar outpost safely. Relatively new, she doubted Wyatt even knew about it. Like the Cotton family, the Greenbriars had been around for generations, leading hikes and capitalizing on the history and natural benefits of the Black Hills.

Snow, without the constant driving wind, made the hike feel almost idyllic. Two old friends—old lovers—taking time to enjoy a quiet walk through a gorgeous snow-covered landscape. There were miracles and worlds caught between every tree and wind-driven drift.

In some places the accumulation was already above her knees. If it kept coming down and the wind kicked up again who knew how high the drifts could be. They hadn't done anything like this since they were kids.

"You know they might not survive," she said, breaking the comfortable silence. Wyatt had taken a few minutes to backtrack to the place he'd last seen Cordell. From what he could tell, the other two men had continued on toward the shelter of the museum. "Too easy to get lost."

"I'm aware."

"What will the FBI do about that?"

"To me?"

She nodded. Wyatt shouldn't be penalized for anything that had gone wrong since the robbery. These conditions rendered any plan useless and, unless she was mistaken, the weather would get worse again before the storm moved on.

"If they die and the diamonds and bodies are recovered, the FBI might hold up their end of the deal," he said.

His tone didn't sound overwhelmingly certain. "And if they escape?"

"Well, that could be a more serious problem for me," he admitted. "There is a paper trail to backup that I was sent here to work undercover. That should prevent any legal issues. I don't have a prior criminal record or the diamonds, so they can't keep me on the hook."

Naturally, he'd left a trail, but she wasn't sure if it would be enough. "I do."

"You do what?"

She'd planned to wait until they'd found real shelter, until she was sure she could trust him to tell him everything. But if that conversation and kiss had confirmed anything about her feelings for Wyatt, a part of her would always trust him and see the best in him.

"I have the diamonds," she whispered.

He stopped moving, as if the weather had frozen him

solid. "What?" He rushed forward. "How? I saw you hand the Mae West over to Cordell."

"The accident must've rattled Cordell more than he realized." She held up her gloved hands and wiggled her fingers. "Blame the seasons of dealing poker. I have the Mae West in my pocket, Cordell has Karl's key fob. I swapped it while Baker was arguing about the coat."

"Wow."

Wyatt's obvious pleasure was almost as effective as his kiss at warming her. "I also found a bunch of loose stones Karl had in his pocket before I came to save you."

"Save me?" His eyes sparkled and somewhere behind the scarf, she knew he grinned. "Because I'm not a criminal."

"Save you or possibly arrest you." She shrugged and kept going. Stopping only made it harder to start up again, a sure sign she was losing the current battle against the elements. "Or wring your neck," she added. "Somewhere in all of that mess I decided if anyone was going to hurt you it should be me."

Her thighs were quivering and she wobbled through the next few paces. He hustled up next to her, as if he sensed her distress. "I'm fine," she assured him.

"How much further?" he asked.

She knew he wanted to lead, to carve a path through the snow to make the hike easier for her. She surveyed their surroundings, knowing everything was taking longer because of the storm. "Not far. The sign..."

Her voice trailed off as she turned a slow circle, looking for the marker. The wording would be blotted out, but the shape of the sign, posted high on a tree trunk, should be nearby.

She started to shake and swore at herself as she recognized the signs of dehydration and looming hypothermia. She'd spent too much energy rushing after Wyatt. Sheltering for a time had helped, but without any food or water, the short break hadn't been as effective as she'd hoped.

"Evie?"

The worry in his voice was clear, even if he sounded like he called her name from across a canyon. Snowflakes dropped gently onto her face, tangled in her eyelashes. Had she fallen?

She blinked, or tried to, determined to keep her heavy eyelids open. Then she saw it, the sign jutting out from a tree just over Wyatt's shoulder. She hoisted her hand up, pointing toward the sign. "There." As her vision went from gray to black, she prayed that the word made it past her lips.

WYATT REFUSED to panic as he crouched down and maneuvered Evie's limp body over his shoulder. Gritting his teeth, he pushed to his feet. Steady on his feet, he marched on. So much for Army assessments and standards, he thought. Moving as quickly as the snow allowed, he carried Evie toward the Greenbriar Goldrush. The square building reminded him of the old ghost town Cordell had been aiming for. Fashioned after a classic western general store, there was a wide, raised porch and big display windows up front.

He eased Evie down to the snow-dusted porch floor, supporting her between the wall and his good leg. Despite the old-west facade, the door was modern enough with an electronic lock and keypad panel. He tested the handle anyway and shoved the door with his shoulder, but it held.

"Evie." He patted her ghostly-pale face. Her lips were so blue his heart stuttered. When she'd dropped into the snow... it had happened so fast, but he couldn't think about that now. She was breathing and her pulse was steady. He had to get her inside and warm her up.

"Evie, honey. Do you know the code?" He gave her shoulder a gentle shake.

He'd break a window as a last resort. Although he didn't want to create trouble for the business owners, he really didn't want to compromise the shelter if he didn't have to.

"Wyatt?" She slurred his name and tried to rub at her eyes.

He caught her hands, chafed them with his own. "We're at the Goldrush place. What's the security code?"

"Umm." She squinted at him. "Try 48482," she said through chattering teeth.

The code worked and the lock opened. He dragged her inside and kicked the door closed. Setting the lock once more, he turned his attention to the woman at his feet.

"I might be a poker-dealing popsicle," she muttered.

"Maybe. But you're definitely the sweetest one," he replied. He tried to knock off the snow caked to her pants and quickly gave up. Scooping her into his arms again, he carried her away from any possible drafts near the front door and windows. One side window was already blocked by a snow drift, but enough light filtered through the window at the opposite end of the narrow building for him to find his way.

He tucked her behind the sales counter. "Wait here."

"You think I'm a flight risk?"

Her humor was a good sign, he thought, hurrying away in search of the thermostat. Finding the system, he turned on the heat, praying everything with the system was in working order. The fan kicked on, which was a good sign. Although the shop had been closed up for the winter, there were cases of water stocked in a storage room and plenty of merchandise that could be helpful. He dragged a camp chair and a stack of polar fleece blankets embroidered with the Greenbriar logo behind the counter. He hauled over a case of water too and then started stripping away her frigid, wet clothing.

"Wyatt, relax. I'll be okay. I just need some water and a few minutes to rest."

"That's what you said before you went down like a tree."

"Did I make a sound?"

He shook his head at another attempt at humor. "I was around to hear it, so yeah."

"Good." She tried to help him peel away the layers, but her movements were more clumsy than helpful.

He gently swatted her hands aside. "Let me take care of you, Evie." Kidnapping her hadn't looked like a caring gesture at the time, but it had been the only way to prevent something worse. He wouldn't let the storm steal her away from him now. "Just this once at least."

She subsided, but he suspected they were both grateful he stopped undressing her when he reached the layers of her shirt and underwear. Her legs were chapped and rosy from the cold and soaked fabrics. He covered her in several blankets and then massaged her lightly all over, trying to work some feeling back into her muscles. Gradually the color came back into her lips and he checked her fingertips and toes to make sure she wasn't fighting frostbite.

"The boots were too big, but they did the trick," she said wiggling her toes. "Make sure you take care of yourself too."

He handed her a bottle of water, opening the cap for her and then taking a bottle for himself. They both drank them straight down and he repeated the process for each of them. "I had better gear to start with," he reminded her. Another strike against him for dragging her out here. Still, near frostbite had to beat a bullet on the grand scale.

"Stop beating yourself up, Wyatt."

He aimed a scowl at the fireplace. "Does that thing work?"

"Yes." She caught his hand and laced her fingers through his. "You did what you had to do in the casino, Wyatt. I *know* that."

Her hands were less like blocks of ice and more like the refrigerated case at the grocery. He studied her short fingernails, unable to meet her gaze.

"I'm safe," she continued. "I'll be room temperature soon. Thanks to you."

Emotion clogged his throat. He quickly pushed away from her to find wood for the fire. "I left you at the SUV," he said.

She muttered something surely unflattering. "Because you know I can handle myself. An hour ago you called me indestructible."

"I was working out how to get back to you." A blast of cold air rushed down the chimney when he opened the flue.

"Close it," she snapped. "If you light a fire, the smoke will be a beacon to Tate and Baker."

Crap. He'd been so consumed with her wellbeing he hadn't thought about that. He did as she said and stepped back from the stone hearth.

"Do they sell sleeping bags here?"

"Check the back room," she said. "The family stores some personal gear back there."

He found a sleeping bag and a camp stove with fuel. They could use that instead of a fire to keep warm until the heat system started to make a difference. Past the backroom, there was a kitchenette with canned goods, dishes and a working microwave. At least he could get some hot food into her soon.

"Do I want to know how you know the store code and the personal habits of the Greenbriars?" he asked when he returned, setting the sleeping bag and stove between them.

"Probably not," she admitted from under the heap of blankets.

"Tell me anyway," he suggested. Firmly.

"Fine. A few years ago, there was a merger in the works between Cottonwood and Greenbriar. It fell apart and Dad never let me hear the end of it."

His stomach sank. "What kind of merger?" At her cocked eyebrow he knew. She'd nearly married one of the Greenbriar boys. He bit back a demand to know which one. None of them were good enough for her. No one was. Not even him. But Evie would've done her best to make it work. Anything to keep Cottonwood going.

"Your dad's idea?"

"No." Her fingers tangled together. "Mine. It was one suggestion he didn't shoot down outright," she admitted quietly.

Wyatt surged to his feet, needing some distance. He couldn't picture Evie with another man without a haze of red blotting out the image. She was *his*, though he had zero claim on her. He had no right to be this angry.

"I took the Silver Aces job instead," she said.

He scrubbed at his face and pulled himself together. The close call was news to him, but she'd dealt with all of this alone because he'd stayed away, too afraid to reach out. He lit the camp stove and moved around behind her, stretching out his legs on either side of hers, her back against his chest. She didn't resist, though her body was stiff for a few minutes.

It was penance, he decided. Holding her close, keeping the contact friendly and proper when his mind raced down far more intimate paths. There were so many things he wanted to say, things he should've said eleven years ago.

She relaxed a little at a time as he stroked her hair, until her head was heavy on his shoulder. Her breathing was deep and even and he peeked down to confirm she'd fallen asleep.

"I've loved you all my life, Evelyn Cotton. If I could do it differently I would."

She never would've left her parents and the business to follow his Army career. Maybe, if he'd known how things would turn out, he would've tried harder to find a solution closer to home. Closer to her.

Maybe.

He'd had to get away from the places and habits that ruined his mother and left behind a wasteland where a family had been. Through the years, his memories of Deadwood had turned into a roiling mass of black clouds full of soul-shaking thunder and jagged lightning strikes. He'd stayed away, so certain he couldn't survive a visit.

Eleven years was a long time to search for answers that had been right inside him all along. He'd never missed Deadwood much, but he'd never stopped craving Evie. "I'm sorry I was a jerk," he whispered against her temple. "Then and now."

Once they were clear of this mess he'd sit down with her and tell her how he felt and what he wanted to do about it. With the compensation the FBI had promised him for the capture of the thieves and recovery of the diamonds, he could invest in her business. And keep her from resorting to a marriage for the sake of business capital.

As she slept, he wondered how he was going to leave her when the time came. Did he have to? Was there a solution here that would suit them both?

Despite all his training and service in the Army, he'd never drummed up the courage to come back to his hometown. To Evie. The awareness shamed him. "I'll get us out of this, baby. Then we'll sort out you and me."

Evie woke up in a rush, disoriented and too warm. It was dark and the wind was howling. She tried to wriggle a foot out of the covers, but her legs were wrapped tightly. The pillow under her cheek was hot and there was a firm pressure all along her spine. Where in the world was she?

"Shh. It's just me."

Wyatt. His scent clicked for her even before the words registered. His muscular arm was the hot pillow under her cheek. In some deep part of her Wyatt would always equal safety and comfort, even after he'd broken her heart. The day came back to her and she remembered how he'd rescued her when her body temperature had dropped and she'd run out of fight.

"When did you tuck us into the sleeping bag?"

"Shortly before my feet turned into blocks of ice." He shifted around and loosened the blankets. "Better?"

"Definitely less like a mummy, yes. Thanks."

"Hungry?"

"Famished." Her stomach rumbled, confirming her answer. "You didn't eat?"

"I was busy with other things." He reached over and turned on an LED lantern.

She felt a little guilty. "I fell asleep on you."

"Best thing you could've done." He handed her another bottle of water. "Drink up."

"In a minute." After hiking through the blizzard in less than ideal gear, she'd never thought she'd be too warm again, but the cool air on her bare legs felt good. Refreshing. Energizing. Deliberately ignoring the embarrassing fact that she wasn't fully dressed, she darted down the hall to the restroom. On her way back to their indoor campsite behind the sales counter, she noticed he had their clothes hanging up near an air vent to dry. She checked the pockets inside the coat and discovered the diamonds were still there.

She touched the pants, still damp, and shivered at the idea of wearing those layers again. It was probably wrong to hope Tate and Baker had been overcome by the storm and wouldn't threaten or rob anyone ever again.

"Here." Wyatt folded a blanket in half and wrapped it around her waist. "You don't need to get chilled again."

"Too late," she said. "I was thinking about Tate and Baker."

"Forget them. If they followed my advice, they're safe enough at the mining museum."

"Is it wrong of me to hope they didn't make it?" Wrapped in the blanket, she shuffled along as he went into the kitchenette. "So what now? Do you call the FBI and tell them where they can pick up the loser duo?"

"The FBI is grounded," he said. "They can't move until the storm passes." He put a cup of soup in the microwave and punched the buttons, refusing to look at her.

"No," she said, suddenly understanding what he was considering. "You can't go up against them alone."

He was searching the cabinets. "I'm definitely not taking you."

The arrogant tone lanced through her. All the warm intimacy of the past hours, his care and comfort, the sweet familiarity of having her best friend back in her life, soured. She'd lived here, invested her money and her soul in the community over the past eleven years. The robbery was a personal affront, Cordell and his crew a blight on the community. She wouldn't let Wyatt leave her out now.

A growl rose in her throat as he set the cup of steaming soup in front of her. With a show of wisdom, he backed away. "Evie, you passed out a few hours ago."

She spooned up soup, inhaling the savory aroma. "I didn't have the right gear." She sipped the broth, let the heat slide down her throat. "I was dehydrated. Both problems can be solved now."

"You've been through—"

She cut him off with a sharp look. "Everyone's been through stuff. Me. You." She paused as he brought his own cup of soup to the small table. "Maybe some food will restore your common sense."

He frowned into the wisp of steam rising from the cheery red and white container.

The silence wasn't so friendly this time, the only sounds breaking the tension were the wind buffeting the building outside and the softer sounds of two people enjoying hot soup. Somewhere in the fog of her hypothermia, she remembered the touch of those lips against her hair, the delicate skin of her temple. He'd demonstrated such care after shocking her at the casino.

"Without me, where would you have spent the night?" she asked.

His lips twisted a grim resignation in his eyes. "With Cordell and Baker, wherever we could have survived until the meet."

"Wyatt, he held a gun to your head."

"He's not the first," Wyatt replied too easily.

She tensed from head to toe, a far different kind of chill moving over her skin. How could he be so cavalier about his life? He *meant* something to her. Regardless of what tomorrow held, she wouldn't let him throw his life away. "That's no excuse to leave yourself open to a worst-case scenario."

"No room for worst-case. I'm here with you." He drank more water, then set the bottle down, his face serious. "I'm thinking any reward money I get should go to you." He leaned forward, determination in his blue eyes. "I could be the right investor for Cottonwood."

"Reparations?"

He nodded, still not meeting her gaze.

"So if you don't survive an encounter with Tate and Baker, how does that work for me? I'll just waltz into the nearest FBI office, drop the diamonds on the desk and tell them you sent me to collect?"

"Actually, that could work," he said with a smile. "With either the casino or the FBI. The casino security footage would support your claim. You'd have the money to invest in your business."

"Oh." Her fingers dug into the blanket keeping her legs warm. She might wring his neck after all, if he didn't give up this idea of becoming a martyr for her.

She recognized this side of Wyatt. Should've expected this kind of reaction. When they were kids, he tried to fix his mother's mistakes, to cover for her. He would throw himself into the sport of the season, apply himself to school work, or find odd jobs to keep himself busy. To make himself valuable, as if every good thing he did could erase the stain of her addiction and neglect.

Until this moment, Evie had never felt like one of his projects. The grief of his sudden departure, the rejection and self-doubt she'd endured in that hollow aftermath was better than being put into a box for Wyatt's higher purpose. She wouldn't let him get away with doing it now. Not with her.

He'd made choices and eventually life had brought him back to Deadwood. She'd dealt with her emotional road-blocks in his absence. It was time for them to clear the air and redefine how things would work between them now.

"You can fix it all." She was on her feet before she realized she'd moved. "That's great, if you want to be the hero of the world—live or die—but don't think I'm going to sit right here batting my eyelashes and being grateful."

That got his attention. He looked up, heat burning in his

blue eyes. "You don't have to be grateful. I don't recall asking for your thanks."

"No, you didn't ask for anything. That's the problem." With all the dignity she could muster in her current state of dishevelment, she collected her disposable soup cup and spoon and carried them to the trash. "You probably just *assume* I'll give your damn eulogy."

"You're overreacting."

The word hung there between them. Now she was hot all over. Hot enough to probably melt the first foot of snow pressed up against the window if she touched the glass.

"Caring about the welfare of someone I *love* is not overreacting. Think about it, Wyatt. You're boxing me up and pushing me away. Again. It's just another verse of the sad song you played eleven years ago. A man has a serious problem when he'd rather risk death than face his feelings."

He shoved back from the table and stalked over to her. "How am I the bad guy because I want to keep the woman *I* love out of harm's way?"

It should have been elation coursing through her at his declaration, instead it was a stomach-dropping dread. Eleven years ago he'd told her he loved her and he'd walked away without a word. He gripped her shoulders, his gaze drilling into her, through her. She felt more vulnerable with him right now than she had when the SUV had slid off the road.

"The robbery, the crash, nearly killed me." She felt the distinct pressure of every single fingertip as she watched him gather his thoughts. "Not the weather or the car or even Cordell's stupid guns. You. You at risk, in jeopardy because of me. I can't bear that again, Evie."

"Well man up," she managed. "You need someone to watch your back. Someone who can navigate through a little snow."

He closed his eyes and his hands fell away. Then he tipped

his head to the ceiling, exposing that strong column of his throat as he laughed bitterly. "Only you would call the worst storm in history a little snow."

Was he giving in? She couldn't tell. It had never been easy to win an argument with Wyatt.

Her fingers itched to touch him, not with anger or frustration. No, he made her long for the heat of his skin, the rasp of his whiskers and the sensual promise in every firm muscle of the man he'd become.

"We'll leave the diamonds here," she suggested, pressing what she chose to believe was a momentary advantage. "You said Baker was injured. We can do this."

He shook his head and swore. "I forgot you had the diamonds. Once Cordell figures out his take is short he'll come unhinged." Wyatt's eyes were full of worry again. "I know you want to help me, but you don't know him like I do."

"He doesn't know me either. He doesn't know *us*." She realized that having this discussion while she was wrapped in a blanket wasn't helping her cause. She tossed the covering over the back of a chair and stalked down the hall toward the storage area. Although they didn't carry a full line of outerwear for sale, she knew the Greenbriars kept the back room stocked for personal use.

"You sure got comfortable with their operation," Wyatt observed from the doorway as she helped herself to silk underwear, a sweater, two pairs of thick socks, water-resistant pants and better-fitting boots.

"Part of the near-merger." She kept her voice neutral as she wriggled into the warm clothing. "You used to like the Greenbriars."

"That was before I knew you wanted to marry one of them."

"Wanted is definitely overstating it. It was business." She

shot him a look, enjoying the thrill of the possessive gleam in his gaze. "This stash is mostly for emergencies for staff, customers, or search and rescue efforts. You remember how those go."

"Yeah. I'd rather we didn't add to those statistics." He was at her back again, crowding her as he examined the supply closet. "You won't even think of staying behind?"

She turned within the framework of his arms, sparkles of need lighting her up inside. He may not want to admit it, but he needed her. Survive first, then deal with the rest of their unfinished business. "Did that approach work for you after the crash?"

"That was different." His gaze dropped to her mouth. "I believed you'd go for help."

She licked her lips. "Convinced yourself is more accurate."

His mouth crashed to hers and those big hands pulled her tightly against his hard body. She couldn't decide if there were too many or too few layers between them. Her hands slid under his shirts, gliding over the defined ridges of his taut abs.

Her blood positively sizzled in her veins. She'd missed this intensity, this intimacy so much. No one else had ever stirred her like Wyatt. Maybe this would become a closure kiss or a what-if kiss, but she didn't care. It was a right-now kiss and she locked into the moment.

What they'd been to each other as kids, the potential for more tempted her beyond reason. She wasn't letting him go without a fight.

He cupped her face, tunneled his hands into her hair, tipping her mouth to the perfect angle. She couldn't resist him. Had never wanted to. They were good together, at school, at work, and at this.

She smoothed her hands along his spine, her fingers

digging in when he nuzzled that sensitive spot on her neck. With a chuckle, he brought his forehead to hers.

They'd exchanged versions of 'I love you', words she'd never given to another man, and yet the ramifications had to wait until Cordell was contained.

"Please stay here," he whispered.

"Only if you stay here with me," she countered.

"Mule."

"Ass." She softened the insult with a fast kiss and a squeeze of his backside before she slipped out of his arms.

She found a sweater and they both chose better cold-weather gear. Wyatt gathered a coil of rope and a hunting knife too.

"Flare gun?" he asked.

"No one would see it," she reminded him. She emptied the pockets of Karl's coat onto the front counter. "Here are the diamonds." He walked up beside her and stared down at the massive Mae West Solitaire, giving a low whistle. Even the low light from the window set the gems on fire, the stones casting that fire across the walls and ceiling. Across his striking face.

"They'll be safer here," she said, dragging her thoughts back on track.

"We might need the leverage," he said. "Above all, Cordell is greedy."

She believed him. "They sure dress up a space." Her gaze followed the colorful refracted light. "How did he plan to liquidate them?"

"I'm sure he has a fence lined up," Wyatt said. "He paid me a few grand up front, and the rest was supposed to hit my account within a week of his escape. That's all up to the FBI now. I just want him out of Deadwood and far away from you."

She tipped one of the larger stones from Karl's stash back

and forth on the countertop. "Would you have come to see me? Be honest," she added, without looking at him. She didn't want to believe their new connection was completely a coincidence or a byproduct of an attempt to stop a thief.

Behind her, he sighed. "No. Yes. Probably no," he amended. She caught him scrubbing at the stubble on his jaw and she wished they could go back to kissing. "I'd hoped to get in and out of town without seeing you," he admitted. "But seeing you now, I know I couldn't have left without checking in."

Love was a multi-faceted pain in the butt, she thought. Chip away at one side and something else emerged. She gathered up the smaller diamonds for safekeeping and zipped them into her pocket. Going back to the storeroom, she found another sock to protect the Mae West and zipped that outrageous stone into a different pocket.

"I never wanted you to get hurt," he said. "Then or now."

She nodded, once. "I'm sorry."

"What do you have to apologize for?"

She shrugged. "The years we lost. My bitterness over it." She met his gaze. "All of the very dark thoughts I've aimed at you recently."

He grinned. "Pretty sure I deserved every one of those dark thoughts."

"Oh, you did." She laughed, then braced against the counter to get her boots on. "Tell me what you have in mind for corralling Cordell."

"Their only smart move was to go on to the mining museum. With luck they're snowed in."

"We haven't checked." She glanced toward the window. "Odds are good we might be too."

He grimaced. "We'll find a way out, but how do we get to the museum without snowshoes?"

"I was thinking we'd use the snowmobile in the shed."

"What?"

"See?" She grinned at him, delighted to surprise him. "You do need me."

"Every damn day," he admitted. "But I'm driving."

She cocked an eyebrow, stared him down.

"Fine. You can drive, but only until we're close. The best play is for me to go in alone, while you cover me from a distance."

"And what can I do from a distance?" she asked.

"Keep watch, take pictures." He handed her his cell phone. "Call it in if you can get a signal. There's all kinds of ways to be helpful."

"*Mm-hm.*" She planted her hands on her hips. "I'll take that as an opening list. I reserve the right to step in as needed."

"I can't talk you out of that?"

"We're a team or we're not," she said. She was zipping up her coat when she heard the whine of a snowmobile. "You hear that?" she asked. He nodded. "It has to be Cordell." There wasn't a single, legitimate reason for anyone to be out in this weather.

Wyatt darted across the room to the front window, then peered through the side window that wasn't covered with ice and snow. "No visibility," he stated. "Are there any weapons stashed around here that you haven't mentioned?" he asked.

"There has to be a shotgun or rifle around here." She dropped down to search the shelves under the counter while Wyatt searched the back rooms. "Nothing," he said, coming back in. "I hate to think what that man did to get a snowmobile."

"Grab the keys," she murmured. "The mining museum has undergone a facelift in recent years." He'd know that if he'd ever come back. "A building remodel, new tours, maps and posters, along with equipment including, but not limited to, hosting a snowmobile club and garage. Really, my dad is the only one averse to progress these days. Everyone is doing cross-promotion."

"That's how he found us," Wyatt grumbled. "I didn't know he could read a map without an assistant."

"Joke later," she said. "Do we wait him out or what? He can't be sure we're in here." Thank goodness he hadn't built a fire. While the wind whipped everything into a blur, the scent of a fire out here would've made Cordell's search easier.

"I should've taken a look around earlier," Wyatt chided himself.

"And left tracks in the snow? That would've only clued him in faster." She made sure the camp stove was cold and turned off the lantern. "Come on. We'll take the back door," she said with confidence. "It's closer to the shed." She tossed him the snowmobile keys.

He caught them and led the way down the hallway. At the back door, Wyatt unlocked the deadbolt and stepped in front of her again. Did he expect her to step outside and invite Cordell to shoot? When would he get it through his thick skull that she didn't want to see him get hurt either?

They stood there together, listening as the snowmobile passed close to the building and around to the front of the store. The sound died, followed quickly by heavy footsteps on the front porch. She supposed it was too much to hope they were wrong and the snowmobile was part of a search and rescue party.

Wyatt scowled, his finger over his lips.

Any hope that the visitor might be friendly was dashed when two loud gunshots reverberated through the building.

"Jameson!"

Hearing Cordell's shout, Wyatt turned the knob and put his shoulder to the back door, but it didn't give more than an inch. Snow sifted in around their feet. This exit route was blocked.

Evie started for the window with the least amount of snow, backpedaling when a shadow approached from the other side.

"It's them," Baker's voice carried from the other side of the glass.

Behind her, Wyatt swore.

"Jameson, get out here. We need to talk." Tate's voice slithered over her skin.

She pulled Wyatt toward the storage room. "Hold the door," she ordered.

Wyatt cursed. "We're trapped, Evie."

She didn't waste time with a reply. She pulled a rolling ladder into place and scrambled up to open the attic access door. "Hurry."

Wyatt followed her, kicking the ladder back as he ducked inside. "Really trapped," he said as Tate crashed into the store, shouting and swearing.

He tugged on his hood and twisted around to crawl after her. Being smaller, she had an easier time scooting around the boxes of seasonal stock and decorations toward the window at the end of the long, narrow space, but he stayed close.

She covered her face and kicked through the glass, then threw herself outside.

"Evie!"

Wyatt's shout followed her as she slipped down the roof of the covered porch. Baker was waiting for her, but she'd been counting on that. If they could make their stand here, somehow contain the thieves until the weather cleared, they might have a chance.

Not just a chance to survive Tate's revenge or the blizzard, but a chance to be together again. That hope propelled her as Baker tackled her, the force driving her into a deep snowdrift.

She writhed beneath him, though there wasn't much room with the snow pinning her in on all sides. Blocking his attempts to get his hands around her throat, she was grateful for the necessary gear that impeded his efforts.

Suddenly, instead of Baker filling her vision, she was looking up into snow-covered trees framing an overcast sky full of clouds. She scrambled out of the snowdrift to see Wyatt squaring off with Baker.

"Get the snowmobile!" Wyatt shouted as he dodged a punch.

Her first instinct was the Greenbriar machine. Looking to the shed, she saw the drift covering two thirds of the door. They'd never get to it before Tate shot them both. Then she heard the revving engine of the snowmobile around front. She'd scold herself later, if she survived.

Tate rounded the corner of the store, the back end of the machine fishtailing behind him. Inexperience and desperation made him reckless. He immediately dismissed her, aiming the machine at Wyatt.

She screamed a warning.

Wyatt must have heard her, but it was too late.

His body twisted, not quite in time, his face registering shock as he was bumped aside. Baker fell the other way, taking a face full of snow as Tate turned. His expression was stark hatred and vindictiveness as he circled around and aimed the machine at her.

Behind him, Wyatt was getting to his feet and Baker was stumbling, holding his side. Wyatt had to be okay. She clung to that singular thought, unable to comprehend another outcome.

She moved straight toward Tate and at the last second threw herself at the nearest tree, taking a stand in the rutted path left behind by the snowmobile's runners. Looking around for a fallen limb she could use as a weapon, she came up empty, the snow was too deep.

"Stay away from him," she shouted at Baker when he stumbled toward Wyatt. Baker didn't look like he could be much of a threat, but she wasn't taking any chances.

Tate muscled the snowmobile around and was taking aim at her once more. She fumbled with her zipper and used her teeth to pull off a glove so she could reach into her pocket. Circling the tree, forcing Tate to recalculate his angle again, she pulled out a few of the loose diamonds and threw them at his face as he passed her.

"Lose something?" she shouted over the drone of the engine. Her fingers were shaking from the freezing air and the barely leashed panic coursing through her veins.

Tate cursed her, standing up on the snowmobile and leaning forward as he came at her once more.

What she wouldn't give for one well-placed rock, covered by snow, that would pitch him over and knock him out. Then she realized she had all the rocks she needed. She reached into her pocket and pulled out another diamond, pretending to hold something larger.

She raised her hand and threw a strike of epic proportions.

Tate shrieked and jumped off the snowmobile, running in the direction of her toss. His movements were awkward as his feet sank into the snow, his arms flailing for balance.

She smiled. *Gotcha*. She plucked out a few more diamonds, tossing them to either side of him.

He reached out as if he could catch one of the precious gems before it was lost in the snow. Of course, he missed. On his knees, he dug through the snow. "Stop! Stop!"

"I'll give you the Mae West if you hand over your gun and leave right now," she offered.

"Yes." He reached for his gun.

"Slowly," she warned, hand poised near her pocket. "Throw it over your shoulder."

He did as she asked. "Thank you. Now get the hell out of here." She secured the pouch of remaining diamonds. "Without a guide."

"We'll get lost."

"Not my problem." She figured the bears would enjoy a convenient, if somewhat stale snack when they woke up in the spring. Provided the authorities didn't find his lousy carcass first.

Tate's gaze narrowed, mean and calculating, as he got back on his feet. "I'll just take you and—"

The threat was smothered by the snow as Wyatt shoved him down, face first, and dropped his knee hard between the man's shoulders. The fight was over that fast. Wyatt gave him just enough room to grab a shallow breath.

"You're a better man than me," she groused.

Wyatt laughed. "Get the rope."

"You know what I mean," she said with a snort as she realized what she'd said. "He doesn't deserve it."

"Maybe not, but neither of us deserve to have his blood on our hands."

She studied him for a long moment, seeing the boy he'd been and the man he'd become. He'd gone to grim places and carried out orders she couldn't even fathom. Didn't want to. Even if he'd never planned to return to Deadwood she was grateful he was here now. Thankful he was a hero at heart.

"What happened to Baker?" she asked.

"He's passed out. Injury, exertion or whatever." Beneath Wyatt, Cordell's muffled voice sounded worried. "He's not dead, but he can't fight. Are there any diamonds left in there?" he queried.

Tate tried to talk again.

"Plenty." She smiled. "We need to confiscate the diamonds

he has," she said. A gust of wind lifted the top-most layer of snow, carving from one drift to add to another. "Wind is changing," she said. "Maybe the worst of this storm is over."

"Let's get them secured and see if we can get out a call for help."

"On it." She trudged back toward the outpost for the rope and whatever else might keep Tate and Baker subdued. "Then we'll talk," she added once she was out of earshot.

She wouldn't let this prime opportunity for a second chance with Wyatt pass her by.

CHAPTER TEN

After a brief debate, Wyatt and Evie decided to keep Tate and Baker in the outpost. They built up a fire in the hearth and gave the men a couple of blankets and some bottled water while they debated what to do next. It would be so nice to leave them here to rot but that wasn't practical and most likely the FBI would frown upon it too. Not to mention the mess it would leave for the Greenbriar's to clean up.

The snowmobile from the mining museum had a radio, but it was broken.

"You'll need to go back to town," he said. "You can lead Sheriff Russell in to pick us all up."

"Not without you," she argued.

He almost smiled, she was so predictably stubborn. "No one but the FBI knows I'm not part of Cordell's crew and there's no way to know if they've revealed themselves to the sheriff." Her brow furrowed, but he knew he was getting through. "They all think I'm a kidnapper. It will be faster all around if you go alone."

She stalked past him and into the outpost. He followed, laughing to himself when he caught her checking their restraints. "You shouldn't be alone with them," she said once she was back outside.

"Have a little faith," he said.

She pressed her lips together, clearly holding something back. He didn't know she was capable of that. Climbing into the seat, she gave him a tight smile. "Don't do anything stupid while I'm gone."

She drove off before he could kiss her and he stood there, listening to the whine of the engine long after she was out of sight. He didn't go back inside, too afraid of haranguing or hurting Cordell. The man had nearly killed Evie more than once. He needed the reward money and to get that, he needed to do this the right way.

Waiting with his own thoughts wasn't any easier than dealing with Cordell and Baker would have been. As the adrenaline drained away, he couldn't stop thinking about all of the ways he'd gone wrong with Evie. He'd been a kid, sure. Scared of his mother's addiction dragging him down and Evie too, by association. He'd had to get out.

That was what he wanted to talk about. He wanted to look into her beautiful gray eyes and watch her accept his promise that he'd never walk away again. Returning to Deadwood for the FBI, for his future, had been a choice that he'd instinctively known would give him that opportunity. He finally felt man enough to come back into Evie's orbit. Although he would have been happier if she'd never been caught up in Cordell's mess, he wouldn't have survived this half as well without her.

She was it for him. Somehow he had to find a way to win her back. Her trust, her love, her kisses. Every ounce of the chemistry he remembered was still there between them. He saw it simmering between her flashes of familiar temper and even more tempting tenderness. No one in his life had ever demonstrated such caring and tough love for him in as Evie.

At last the sounds of rescue approached in the form of snowmobiles gliding over the snow-blanketed terrain. It shouldn't have surprised him that Evie led the way. She parked at the far side of the building and sat there, watching the proceedings as the sheriff and Agent Pickering marched Cordell and Baker out.

"Good enough?" he asked Agent Pickering.

"Did you talk to them?"

He shook his head. "Didn't trust myself," he replied. "Is it okay if I ride back with Evelyn?"

Pickering arched an eyebrow and gave him a subtle nod. "As long as you're right behind us. We need full statements, the sooner the better."

He bounded through the snow toward Evie. "You and me."

"That works." She smiled, scooting back to let him drive the snowmobile.

"Did you turn over the diamonds?" he asked before he started the machine.

"Yes." She rolled her eyes. "Everyone acts like I saved a kid." She pulled her scarf up to cover her nose and mouth.

Another chance to kiss her gone. He needed to stop missing those. "The Mae West Solitaire isn't that big," he joked.

"Right?"

"You're the new hometown hero," he said.

She shrugged. "We'll see," she said from behind her scarf. "I think it's too soon for a changing of the guard."

The comment left him wondering what she'd told the sheriff and others before they came back out. Her arms came around his waist and he relished the feel of her pressed up against him.

They needed to talk. It was past time he laid all his cards on the table and let her make an informed decision.

When they reached the casino, the last to join the authorities gathered in the staging area, he quickly realized she hadn't been exaggerating about the general sense of celebration and gratitude. They were surrounded by pleased officials. Everyone from the FBI to the casino security staff were eager to greet them and praise them for bringing in Cordell and Baker.

Now that the FBI had clarified his role in the robbery a weight lifted from his shoulders. He walked with his head high as he and Evie were ushered inside and through back hallways to the rooms set up for the teams investigating the security guard's death and the diamond heist.

Although it was standard procedure, he nearly argued when they were separated to give their statements. He wanted to assure her he wasn't going to disappear again. When they were finally done with the obligations, he sought out Evie for a quick word.

"Your dad was probably worried sick. Have you talked with him? Is someone taking you home?"

"We did talk," she said with a tired smile. "Relief is an understatement. He says the driveway is blocked by a ten-foot snowdrift. I'll stay here. The casino is so delighted to have the diamonds back they're comping me a room." She leaned close so no one else could hear. "A suite, if you can believe it, with all the benefits they save for the whales."

"Nice. Enjoy it." He knew the casino would give her a cash reward as well, but it wasn't his place to tell her. Instead, he indulged in a brief fantasy of having Evie all to himself in that suite, with no cares or crises.

"You could join me."

He tipped his head toward the FBI agents looming behind him. "I'm not done yet, but I'll be in touch soon." And when he did see her again, he'd tell her everything. Ask for everything. His heart stuttered, a combination of anxiety and eagerness.

"Soon," she echoed. Her gaze turned cool and shrewd as if she could see straight through his skin to his rowdy pulse. "Wyatt Jameson, if you leave again without saying goodbye I will hunt you down and make you regret it."

He believed her. "It's not like that," he said. "I just have to take care of a couple of details. I'll be right behind you."

"Promise?"

Damn. After everything past and present, she still trusted he would keep his word. That slayed him. "Evie." He caught her up into a hug, startling them both with how tightly he clung. "I promise," he whispered into her hair.

There was no leaving without saying goodbye now. Where that should've left him uptight and irritable, he found a softness in the promise made. Hell, she didn't know it yet, but there was no leaving. Not as long as Evie remained in Deadwood.

He had a second chance to restore their friendship, a golden opportunity to ask her to build a life with him. He wouldn't screw it up.

APPARENTLY SAVING the Mae West Solitaire warranted a hero's reward. The casino promised Evie a cash reward equal to a percentage of the diamond's value. It was more than enough to bail out her business and set them up for the future, assuming she stayed in Deadwood. The casino also treated her to one of their most luxurious suites, providing everything she could imagine to not only thaw out, but to pamper herself as she recovered from the ordeal. She spent a brief eternity indulging in the steam shower. When she finally turned off the taps and toweled off, she smoothed a silky citrus-scented lotion all over her weary skin. The fragrance gave her mind and heart a bright boost as she wrapped herself in the soft hotel robe.

Someone had delivered a bag of brand new clothes, including shirts and a jacket with the Silver Aces logo. The spa services menu was also prominently displayed, along with a handwritten note from Jack encouraging her to take full advantage of every option. A carafe of hot chocolate had been set out on the table along with two ceramic mugs and platters of sweet and savory treats from the kitchen. Everything looked and smelled so good, so revitalizing, that she felt almost like a princess in a fairy tale.

She hoped Wyatt would enjoy the same indulgent treatment once the FBI was done with him. Agent Pickering had taken her statement quickly and sent her up here to recover before meeting with Wyatt. It was only logical, considering his undercover role with Tate's crew, but she felt sorry for him anyway.

Curling up into a cozy chair with a mug of hot chocolate and half of an oversized peanut butter cookie, she turned on the television. It seemed up here in the hotel, unlike the casino floor, reality was all-too-accessible. Every station was nattering on about the recovered diamonds, the weather system moving out at last, and the capture of Cordell and his crew.

She didn't feel like a hero. There was no cause to feel like a victim, since her old—and once again current—best friend had been the one to take her hostage. She didn't even feel much like a dedicated employee to use the term the reporters preferred. No, she felt like a woman who wanted to sit down with the men in her life and figure out how to move forward.

Hopefully together. At the very least with a comfortable understanding.

Was it time to leave Deadwood? Assuming Wyatt wanted

her tagging along, she could help him set up his new business. The idea of spending time with him, loving him as a friend and partner and building a life warmed her more thoroughly than the shower had. The distance might actually help her relationship with her dad and give her a fresh perspective on her personal goals.

But that potential scenario assumed Wyatt would want that same time with her now that the crisis was over. Although she felt hopeful, she couldn't bank on it.

Her body ached too much to sit still for long. Standing, she crossed to the window, sipping her hot chocolate and burrowing into the robe. Twilight was deepening and waves of untouched snow sparkled under the streetlamps. Although the storm was officially over, it would take several days for the city to dig out and return to normal. Knowing her community, people would already be tired of being stuck indoors. By morning, they'd be itching to get out and get moving, even though the accumulation and drifts would make it difficult to go anywhere.

If only Cottonwood Adventures had the gear, she could offer people the outlet they needed. A thought occurred to her as she studied the courtyard below and gently bloomed into a full-fledged idea. What if they organized a snow day for hotel guests and invited the kids and families from the nearby neighborhoods? It would bring wonderful visibility to her business which would be a big benefit whether they decided to sell or expand. And the casino would get bonus points for community engagement. She mulled over the logistics and then reached out to Jack and Sarah to see if the casino had the desire, staff, and resources to pitch in with her last-minute idea.

To her delight, they were excited about the prospect of having a snow adventure day. As the details came together, she called her dad again.

"Evie." He sounded pleased to hear from her though they'd spoken just a few hours ago. "How is the suite?"

"Amazing." She described it to him. "It's not home." Her heart was all too eager to define 'home' as wherever Wyatt landed. She sure hoped that worked out. "I, um, put some things in motion." She explained the plans for the snow day and the casino's swift agreement and contributions in a rush, then waited on pins and needles for his reaction.

"Sweetheart, you're brilliant." The pride came through loud and clear. "When your mom died, I pulled back from the community." He cleared his throat. "I pulled back from you too. It shouldn't have taken a blizzard and an emergency to wake me up. I'm sorry for not making a better effort to see what you wanted for *your* future."

She had to blink back tears. "Thanks, Dad. Is there any way you could make it over here for the event? I could ask Sheriff Russell to send a snowmobile for you."

"I bet he'd do anything for you," Dale laughed, the sound rusty but welcome. "I'll figure it out, don't you worry. I know you and Wyatt are both in one piece, but it sure will be nice to see you with my own eyes."

After the call, she poured more hot chocolate and jotted down notes on the hotel stationery, reworking her priorities for the reward money based on her father's surprising turnaround. She couldn't wait to tell Wyatt about the snow party plans.

Even with this event stirring ideas for many more, she could happily leave Deadwood if that's what Wyatt needed. But now she wondered if maybe it would be better for him to stay here and reclaim his place as a hometown kid who'd done well despite a rough start.

How crazy that so much had changed in a matter of days, opening up doors her mind and heart had slammed shut. She couldn't recall the last time she'd had so many options. Unless Wyatt didn't want her after all.

She cut off that unsettling thought in a hurry. That was fear talking. Fear that the high of surviving Cordell and reconnecting with Wyatt wouldn't last. Experience had proven to her time and again that it was possible to love someone, to care so deeply about their happiness, and still make choices that severed those ties rather than strengthen them.

Her recent communication challenges with her father and the mistakes Wyatt had made at eighteen were more evidence. No, they weren't eighteen anymore, but she couldn't expect a new relationship to be perfect. Love was work at any age. It had to be a choice. Having made her choice, it was going to be difficult not to push Wyatt into a choice that aligned with hers. But unless he came around on his own, it would never work.

A knock on her door interrupted her thoughts and she hurried to answer. Anything to stop over-analyzing every random thought that popped into her head. Putting her eye to the peephole, her heart danced to see Wyatt and sank when she noticed Agent Pickering was with him.

Her stomach twisted with worry as she opened the door. "Come in," she said, brazening through the fact that she was still in the cushy robe. When he'd said he'd come to her as soon as he could, she thought he'd meant alone.

Whatever they'd been doing, Wyatt had cleaned up and changed clothes. He looked handsome in dark blue jeans and topped with a button-down shirt and a Silver Aces zip-up jacket. His smile sent a tingle through her system. Yeah, she really should've dressed.

"Are you feeling okay?"

"Yes," she said quickly. "Just too lazy to dress yet." She

tilted her head and grinned. "Did you just buy the outfit displayed on the mannequin downstairs?"

His smile lit up his gorgeous eyes. "Pretty much." He plucked at the jacket zipper. "Or rather the FBI did. The casino confiscated everything in my room after the robbery, so..."

She started toward the phone. "They should have returned all that by now."

"The casino is handling it," Pickering said. "We've cleared up his role in the incident."

Incident. What a weak word for what Cordell had put them through.

"We need to tie up a few loose ends and he wouldn't leave without talking to you first," Pickering said. "Is this hot chocolate?" She sniffed at the carafe.

"Help yourself." Evie couldn't tear her gaze away from Wyatt. "Loose ends?" That must mean the team waiting for Tate and the others at the ghost town. She wrapped her arms tight around her middle while she waited for him to confirm her worst fears. They were both well aware that the roads in and out wouldn't be clear. They were asking him to risk too much, too soon.

"Are you even warm yet?" She couldn't hide her worry.

"I'm fine."

His gentle expression forced her to take a step back. She wasn't used to anyone reading her so easily. It was almost as if nothing had changed despite all the years between them. He caught her by the elbow and gently drew her a few paces from Pickering. His touch familiar, comforting.

"Evie," he said softly. "It'll be all right."

"I know." Of course, it would be all right. Cordell's escape team was waiting in a dilapidated collection of deserted and condemned buildings. How hard could it be to round them up?

"Cordell is cooperating," Wyatt said. "They both say Karl killed Stan," he added quietly.

Of course, he'd remembered how much she wanted justice for her friend. "Do you believe them?"

"Yes. The stories line up and frankly, they're too exhausted to lie well." His gaze drifted to Pickering. "I should get going." He shoved his hands into his pockets. "Cordell's getaway guys are sitting ducks. The FBI and the sheriff's team will be doing the hard work," he assured her. "I'm just guiding them in to take down a couple of city boys who probably can't handle their four-wheel drive out here. We can't lose."

City boys armed with guns and radios if they worked with Cordell. "They must have heard by now that the robbery failed."

"Probably," he admitted. "The sheriff parked a team of deputies on the access road, but they can't take down this team alone."

Her hands went cold and her heart stuttered as worry washed over her. It wasn't her place to fuss over him. They were friends. Friends who had shared a few kisses and confessions and no guarantees. They hadn't had a chance to talk about the future, about what a new relationship might look like.

"Evie." He ran his fingertips along the rolled collar of her robe, not quite touching her skin. "I'll be back in a few hours. It'll give you time to get dressed."

She laughed, but her cheeks went hot. Hotter still when Pickering cleared her throat.

"Wait up for me," he said. "I'll bring up champagne to celebrate."

Did that mean what she wanted it to mean?

"Jameson, we need to get moving," Pickering said.

"Give me another minute," he said.

Everything inside her rebelled at the idea of him leaving Deadwood. Irrational but true. A small voice in her head refused to accept he was only heading a few miles north. "Why now? The roads aren't clear," she protested. And why were the authorities so eager to move now when they refused to leave the hotel when Wyatt needed them most?

"They won't wait forever. Cordell convinced them he'd be there before midnight. I'm not going in on my own. I'm just a guide," he repeated. "The take down is a cooperative effort between the sheriff and the FBI. But we have to move now."

It was more dangerous than ever. She chewed on her lip so her concerns couldn't spill out. From the corner of her eye she caught Pickering edging toward the door.

"Jameson," the agent said, "Clock's ticking."

"You'd better go." Did she dare kiss him?

He bent his head and caught her lips in a soft kiss full of promises. A kiss that erased all her doubts. When he eased back, she pressed her fingers to her lips, holding the sensation close.

"I wanted to talk," he said backing away.

That was laughable. "You did not." She crossed her arms over her chest, so her heart wouldn't go flying after him. He said he was coming back. He kissed her like he was coming back. "We will talk, though," she warned.

"I can't wait," he said. His wild grin had only become more irresistible with time. "Your snow day is already a hit. I'll make sure the press is here."

She didn't want to know how he'd manage that. "Be safe. And be smart." She glared past him to Pickering. "I mean it. If you let anything happen to him, you'll answer to me."

"Evie." He rushed across the room and kissed her again. "You're the best. I love you."

Her heart cracked and hope overloaded her system. He meant it. Love glowed in his beautiful blue eyes. She reached deep for one last scrap of courage and realized it was the easiest thing in the world to give him the words that had been carved on her heart years ago. "I love you too." Always. "I never stopped loving you either."

"I knew it." He cradled her face. "Give us a minute," he said to Pickering, his eyes still locked on Evie.

The door opened and closed.

She pressed up on her toes and kissed him, willing all of her heat into him to keep him warm during his next trek through the snow. "Don't you dare get hurt."

"What kind of husband and business partner would that make me?"

She stared up at him. "That doesn't count. When you decide to propose for real, you have to do better."

"Fair enough. I'm not waiting another minute." He dropped to one knee and pulled a small box out of his pocket, holding it up. "This is real. You're my best friend, Evelyn Cotton. You're the only woman I've ever loved. I don't want to spend another hour without you in my life." He opened the box and a stunning, marquis-cut diamond blazed in a cushion of black velvet. "Please make me the happiest man on earth and let me be your husband. By your side, whatever you need, wherever life takes us, no matter how gnarly the trail. Let me be with you forever."

"Oh, Wyatt. Yes. You've always had my heart. Yes to forever with you, wherever we are. Whatever we do." Her knees gave out and she sat down right there on the floor. He slipped the ring onto her finger and she peppered his face with kisses.

Forever had never felt so sweet. "Hurry back," she said as he helped her to her feet once more. She extended her hand, admiring the way the ring sat on her finger and caught the light, straightening it when the loose band slipped.

"Get dressed," he said with that wicked grin. "The jeweler is waiting to size it for you. I'll send up champagne."

She smiled. "The champagne and I will be right here, waiting to welcome you back."

When he walked out Evie did a happy pirouette, thrilled not just about what tonight held, but the bright potential in tomorrow and every day to come.

DEADWOOD 5 NEWS

"And now out to Joyce Adams with a weather update on location today. That looks like quite an undertaking behind you."

"You're right about that, Will." Joyce smiled into the camera. "Although we need to be mindful of the windchill and the reflection off the snow out here, it is wonderful to see the sun shining at last. Winter Storm Holly is marching on toward Minnesota and left us with a blanket of wintery sparkle all over town."

She stepped closer to a cluster of people, red-cheeked and beaming, as a large group of kids worked on a snow fort behind them. "This is Evelyn Cotton and her father Dale of Cottonwood Adventures. They're joined by Wyatt Jameson, Sheriff Russell, and Sarah and Jack, managers of the Silver Aces Casino. Evelyn, can you tell us a bit about what's happening here?"

"Sure. Since schools and most businesses are closed again today, Cottonwood Adventures and the Silver Aces teamed up to host an impromptu snow day celebration."

"How did you get such a big turnout?" Joyce asked.

Evelyn glanced at the others and grinned. "Between the

sheriff's department, social media, and some travelers stranded at the casino with cabin fever, word got around quickly. Everyone was eager to come out and make the best of the situation."

"It has been a difficult couple of days," Joyce agreed. Her face was freezing, but she wanted to get in on the fun before heading back to the studio. "And Wyatt Jameson. Don't tell me our hometown hero is one of those stranded travelers?"

"Not exactly. I did choose the wrong week for my first visit back to Deadwood," he admitted. "But now that I'm retired from the Army, I plan on staying right here."

"You used to work with Cottonwood Adventures, am I right?"

"Yes," he replied. "Back when Evelyn and I were in high school. I'm pleased to be a part of their new expansion plans."

"Maybe this snow party will give the people of Minnesota something to look forward to as they brace for Holly." Joyce turned to Evelyn and Dale and let them plug their business, before getting comments from a few of the kids and adults enjoying the snow party.

"Will, I might take the rest of the day off to play." Joyce handed off her microphone and fell backward into a sparkling-white snow drift to make a snow angel.

At the desk, the evening anchorman laughed at her antics. "You've definitely earned it, Joyce. Thank you."*

Thanks for reading! If you enjoyed this book, please do leave a review.

Read on for a sneak peek of the next STORMWATCH novel, *Snow Brides* by Peggy Webb.

SNEAK PEEK

SNOW BRIDES
STORMWATCH, Book 5
by Peggy Webb

As Stanley Weathers faced the Channel 9 cameras he adjusted his tie and chafed at the latest ribbing he'd taken about his name. It had come from the new hire, some underling in the bowels of the TV station who obviously thought Stan had never heard anybody say, "A weatherman named Weathers? Did you make that up?"

When he got home he'd tell his wife Jean about it, and she'd find a way to make him laugh. *If* he got home. The snowstorm coming their way was a monster beyond anything he'd ever witnessed. He was going to have a hard time maintaining a cool professionalism during the weather report.

"Stan," the cameraman said. "You're on in two."

He put on his stage smile and faced the cameras.

"Holly is her name, and she's unlike any snowstorm we've ever seen." He gestured to the weather map behind him, tracking the storm as he talked. "The blizzard that has held the Northwest in its grip since December 12 is sweeping toward Minnesota. This killer storm has left a path of destruction across Montana, Colorado, Nebraska and South Dakota."

The death toll rose in his mind, and he paused, hoping his TV audience would perceive it as a planned break from his dramatic spiel. Stan was relieved the number of fatalities would be part of the news report, not the weather.

"Expect the blizzard to be one of the worst in the history of Minnesota with snow drifts as high as thirty feet. The mega-monster storm is on a path to hit Grand Marsais at 2:00 p.m. on December 23 and could last up to three days."

There went the big family Christmas. That was the only good thing Stan could say about the storm. Jean had already called to say her parents had sent a text from Atlanta that their flight had been cancelled. He would have enjoyed seeing them, but he couldn't say the same thing about Jean's obnoxious, know-it-all twin sister Joan and her two teenaged brats who were traveling with them.

"Residents are urged to cancel holiday travel plans," he told his TV audience. "Our team here at TV 9 News in Grand Marsais is standing by to bring you a list of airport closings.

As always, Stan the Weatherman will be here at the station bringing you regular updates on Holly. Until then, stay off the roads. Be smart. Be safe."

Chapter 1

December 23
4:00 a.m.

"I should have picked her up."

Joe left his vigil at the window that showed nothing except the distant shape of Carter's Trading Post and the ghostly outlines of security lights that seemed to float above the water in the snow mists swirling through the darkness. A heavy blanket of snow had fallen on Grand Marsais during the night and the temperature had already dropped below zero, both precursors of the blizzard predicted to hit in early afternoon.

Maggie's big chocolate Labrador retriever lifted his head at her husband's uncharacteristic display of nerves then left his pillow by the fire and padded to lean against Joe's leg.

It was uncanny, Jefferson's ability to sense the emotional terrain of his family. Though Maggie shouldn't have been surprised. The four-year-old search and rescue dog had displayed extraordinary intelligence from the moment Maggie started working with him. Even better, he had more heart than any dog she'd ever handled.

He was feeling their pain.

Their daughter Kate was missing, and had been since yesterday afternoon.

"You should have let me go after her," Joe added as he sank onto the sofa, his face etched with worry and defeat.

The worry, Maggie shared, but if she let herself dwell on Joe's sense of defeat and the many reasons why, she wouldn't have the strength to get through this long vigil for her daughter.

"Don't start, Joe."

Hadn't Maggie told herself the same thing a thousand times during the last sixteen hours? Kate, a freshman at the University of Minnesota in Duluth, reveled in her newfound freedom and had scoffed at the idea she couldn't drive a hundred miles north for the holidays.

"Mom!" Even on the phone Kate's most exasperated, long-suffering daughter tone had been evident. "I'll be home long before this so-called monster storm hits."

"You be careful. And start early. Don't wait till the last minute."

"I'm loading the car now. You worry too much, Mom."

That had been nine o'clock yesterday morning. During normal winter conditions snowplows kept the roads between Grand Marsais and Duluth clean. That far in advance of the storm, Kate should have been home before noon, even in holiday traffic.

To make the nightmare even worse, her GPS tracker showed she'd veered far off course. Maggie had been flabbergasted when her daughter's GPS put her in Chicago. And the last time she'd checked, Kate was in Detroit and moving northeast.

A thousand horrors played through Maggie's mind--her daughter skidding off the road and landing in a spot hidden from highway traffic then picked up by a predator who could do anything. Haul Kate out of the country or easily vanish into nearly four million acres of wilderness known as the Superior National Forest. The idea of her daughter in the hands of a predator struck terror to Maggie's soul.

"Don't go there." The sound of her own voice calmed her

a bit, but her mind still spun in all directions.

What if Kate had arranged to meet someone, a guy her parents didn't know, someone she'd met online? It happened all the time, vulnerable young girls with bleeding hearts falling for a sob story only to be lured off then led like lambs to the slaughter.

That didn't sound like something her levelheaded daughter would do, but who knew how she might have changed under the peer pressure on a college campus?

"Joe, I'm going to make a cup of coffee. You want one?"

"No. I'm good."

He wasn't good. Any fool could tell by looking. She wasn't good. *They* weren't good--and hadn't been for a very long time.

She was glad to escape to the kitchen. She popped a pod into the coffeemaker then made the call she didn't want Joe to hear.

Ten years ago he'd have been right with her, taking turns as they called on their network of friends in law enforcement who knew them as two of the most successful search and rescue handlers in the U.S. Now everything about SAR, with the exception of Maggie's dog, sent Joe scrambling backward into a private world of his own making, one with walls so thick and so high Maggie had no hope of getting through.

Longtime friend, Detective Roger Dillard, picked up on the first ring.

"This is Maggie Carter. Any news?"

"Kate has stopped moving. Her GPS tracker shows her in Toronto."

The shock felt as if somebody had drained off all Maggie's oxygen. Coffee forgotten, she sank into a chair.

"That's impossible! She doesn't know anyone there, and she'd *never* go off like that without telling us."

"Are you sure about that? Maybe she had a secret

boyfriend and is planning an elopement. It happens all the time."

"Not with Kate. You know how responsible she is." Roger's daughter Teresa had been one of Kate's best friends since kindergarten. The Johnson's house was her second home. "Something awful has happened. I just know it."

"I've already contacted the authorities in Toronto, Maggie. As soon as they locate her cell phone, I'll let you know."

"You're going to continue your search, aren't you?"

"Of course, I am. I love that kid like she's my own." The line went quiet and Maggie thought she'd dropped the call. Then Roger cleared his throat. "We've already covered a lot of territory north of the college in Duluth, but with the storm closing in, I don't know how long I can keep my men out here."

"You owe me, Roger." This year alone, Maggie had found four missing children for him and dozens of other missing persons through the years, both with her chocolate Lab and the air scent dogs who had come before him.

"I promise we're going to do everything we can to bring Kate home."

"Thanks. I know you will."

Maggie wasn't about to believe her daughter was in Canada.

She was torn between screaming, crying or racing into the night with Jefferson to start her own search. But where to start? Though air scent dogs, unlike tracking dogs, didn't need a last known location for their search, they did need a general area as a starting point. Without one Maggie and her dog would waste precious time randomly plunging into a search in the hundred-mile stretch between college and home. Time she couldn't afford to lose with a blizzard heading their way.

Law enforcement had questioned all the people who saw

Kate last--her roommate, the guard at the campus gate, the owner of the service station just off campus where she always refilled her gas tank before starting home. Kate, the good girl, heeding her dad's advice: Always drive from the top of your tank. You never know what will happen. Driving from the bottom is too risky.

They all remembered her, cheerful, calling out happy holiday greetings and waving as she started toward home. The service station was the last place anyone had seen her, but the manager recalled seeing her drive away and head north.

Maggie grabbed her mobile phone and tapped on her daughter's name in Favorites. How many times did that make since yesterday morning? Ten? Fifteen?

Hi, this is Kate. Leave a message.

"Kate, where are you? If you get this, please, please call me. Even if you've done something you think we won't approve. Your dad and I are worried sick."

Maggie could barely function. The Christmas china she'd dragged out for her daughter's homecoming lunch still sat on holiday placemats, forlorn and hopeless looking among the remnants of a meal they never ate—home baked bread getting hard on the platter, the creamed corn Kate loved, Joe's favorite apple dumplings, his mom's recipe for broccoli salad with cranberries and nuts. The only thing Maggie had rescued from the uneaten meal was her oven roasted turkey. Perfectly cooked, waiting for the meal that was supposed to bring them all back together again, now sitting in its own congealed fat in the refrigerator.

She broke off a piece of bread and nibbled around the edges. Yesterday morning when her life had still been halfway normal, Joe had come into the kitchen while it was baking.

"Something smells good in here."

"Yeast-rising bread. Apple dumplings, too." She pointed to

the casserole dish cooling on the sideboard."

"You've gone all out. Kate bringing somebody home?"

"No. It'll be just the three of us. I want this holiday to be special, Joe. Like it once was."

For a moment he looked gut punched. Then he'd smiled in a pale imitation of the way it used to be. "I think I'd like that."

The one word, *think,* had said more about the state of their marriage than all those nights she'd reached for Joe only to find his side of the bed empty and him sleeping on the sofa with Jefferson on the wool rug beside him.

It had spurred Maggie to take desperate measures. She'd tried to seduce her husband in the kitchen. She didn't care where they landed, the floor, the table, propped against the kitchen sink with the faucets poking into her hips. She'd just wanted proof the spark was still there, no matter how small. She wanted to believe their marriage wasn't dead; it was only in hibernation until some great spring-thaw moment would make it bloom again.

Her spring-thaw moment was a disaster. She'd been clumsy, he'd been awkward, and both of them had been relieved when Maggie's cell phone rang, bringing their pathetic attempt to a halt. He rearranged his clothes while she scrambled for her phone. By the time she found it, she'd missed a call from daughter.

Mom, something's come up. Don't know when I'll get home.

Ten little words. They meant everything and nothing at all.

Kate hadn't answered when Maggie called back. Her daughter's message was the last anybody had heard from her since yesterday morning. And yet, they offered no details. So far search choppers had reported no accidents on the interstate to block traffic, no detours. Why had she called to say she'd be late? Where was she?

Maggie could no longer bear to sit still. She started clearing the table, stowing the clean dishes back into the cupboard, dumping the wilted salad, tossing the corn. The apple dumplings would still be okay. She put them into the refrigerator then grabbed the bread to toss. On second thought, she sliced off the hardened edges then wrapped the soft center in foil.

Joe appeared in the doorway and just stood there saying nothing, his expression speaking volumes. *Everything is gone and I don't know how to get it back.*

Maggie whirled toward him, hands on her hips. "What?"

"Nothing."

"You always say that, Joe. We never talk anymore. Not really."

"What do you want me to say?"

"How about, has Kate told you anything that might give us a clue what's going on?"

"Has she, Maggie?"

Suddenly her legs would no longer support her. She sank into a chair and rested her head on the table.

"Yes," she whispered.

"Yes?" Joe sat down at the table but he didn't reach for her hand, didn't offer her comfort of any kind. "Did you say *yes?*"

An unexpected fury overtook her and she jerked upright to glare at him. "Do you think our daughter's blind? Did you think she wouldn't notice you can hardly bear to be in the same room with me? That every time I head out the door on a SAR mission you hide deeper behind those walls you've built around yourself?"

"I don't even know how to respond to that."

"You can't stand to be home anymore, Joe. You spend more time on the Superior Trail leading guided tours than here."

"What are you getting at?"

"I don't know, I don't *know*." Maggie buried her face in her hands, groaning. If she let herself, she could fall asleep from sheer exhaustion. She forced herself back to life, made herself look at her husband. "Roger says the GPS tracker shows Kate's in Canada."

"That can't be right."

"I told him the same thing. But I keep wondering if she decided at the last minute to spend the holidays with a new college friend."

"She wouldn't do that without telling us."

"Maybe she did." Maggie pulled her cell phone from her pocket to replay her daughter's message. They both strained toward the phone as if they might reach inside and pull Kate to safety. "Maybe the *something* that came up was dread of coming home to parents who don't even seem to like each other anymore, let alone love. Just last week she asked me what was wrong between us."

"Nothing's wrong. And certainly nothing I'd want to discuss with my daughter." Joe shoved out of his chair and stalked off.

For what? To stare out the window? To bundle up and open the trading post?

Nowadays, trouble sent Joe racing toward the comfort of a familiar routine. But she couldn't begrudge him the escape. After all, here she was tidying up the kitchen at four a.m.

The phone she'd left on the table jangled and Roger's number popped up. She seized it as if it were the last life raft on the Titanic.

"Hello."

"Maggie, we've found her car."

"Thank God! Just a minute. I want to get Joe." Maggie raced to the door and yelled for her husband, who came on the run. She punched speakerphone. "Go ahead, Roger."

"Kate's car is in the ditch on a small side road called

Glen's Crossing about sixty-five miles south of Grand Marsais."

The ghost of a memory nagged at Maggie, and she felt the chill of an awful premonition. What was it? She was so tired she couldn't think straight.

"How is she, Roger? Is she okay?"

"She's not here. We found her suitcase in the backseat and a winter parka in the front."

"Kate would never leave the car without a coat," Joe said. "She's a seasoned hiker."

"What about her backpack?" Maggie tried to rein in her fear. More and more it appeared her daughter had been taken.

"We haven't found anything else yet. I've got deputies fanned into the woods searching but the snow last night covered any tracks we might have discovered."

"I'm telling you, Kate wouldn't have left the car," Joe said. "I know that area. It's isolated. There's not a single place nearby where she could have walked in this snow for help, particularly when she could have called us."

"Looks like she had a blowout and the front end of her car is smashed up pretty bad. Considering her GPS tracking information we can't discount kidnapping. I'm still waiting for a call from authorities in Canada."

Dread washed over Maggie, and a premonition so horrible she could almost see her daughter, rendered powerless by evil.

"Something about this whole scenario doesn't feel right, Roger. Give Joe the exact location of the car. I'll be there as soon as I can."

As Maggie raced out of the kitchen she heard Roger firing off directions followed by the caution, "Storm's coming. We don't have much time."

Didn't he think she knew that? The latest weather report

from Stan the weatherman said the massive storm would hit northern Minnesota in ten hours.

Maggie raced into her daughter's bedroom and grabbed the raggedy old Pooh Bear off the bed. Kate had slept with it every night since she was born. The wonder is that she hadn't carried it to college with her. It would hold more of her scent than anything else in the room.

Air scent dogs, unlike tracking dogs, didn't need an article that belonged to the missing. They worked by sniffing the air for the trail everybody leaves behind, unaware--unseen skin cells and hair that float away when you pass through a place, even the gases you exhale when you breathe. Their uncanny olfactory ability was why air scent dogs were so valuable working landslides, avalanches and other freaks of nature and man that buried multiple victims under tons of debris.

Still, the scent-specific object would let Jefferson know beyond a shadow of a doubt he wasn't looking for multiple people. His job was to find Kate.

Kate's bear almost brought Maggie to tears. She hugged the stuffed animal, trying to comfort herself by touching something belonging to her daughter. Finally she said, "Get moving."

It was the sort of advice she'd once given Kate. When you think you can't go one step more, give yourself a pep talk. Out loud.

As she hurried about packing everything she'd need for a SAR search in the dead of winter, possibly in the middle of a blizzard, the memory she'd sought earlier hit her with a force that buckled her knees.

The snow. The location, not twenty miles from Glen's Crossing. The missing girls. Two of them, one year apart. Both college age, both blond. Like Kate.

Maggie had found both of them dead.*

THE STORMWATCH SERIES

Holly, the worst winter storm in eighty years...

Holly blows in with subzero temperatures, ice and snow better measured in feet than in inches, and leaves devastation and destruction in its wake. But, in a storm, the weather isn't the only threat—and those are the stories told in the STORMWATCH series. Track the storm through these six chilling romantic suspense novels:

FROZEN GROUND by Debra Webb, Montana
DEEP FREEZE by Vicki Hinze, Colorado
WIND CHILL by Rita Herron, Nebraska
BLACK ICE by Regan Black, South Dakota
SNOW BRIDES by Peggy Webb, Minnesota
SNOW BLIND by Cindy Gerard, Iowa

Get the Books at Amazon

ABOUT THE AUTHOR

Regan Black, a USA Today bestselling author, writes award-winning, action-packed romantic suspense, paranormal romance, and urban fantasy novels featuring kick-butt heroines and the sexy heroes who fall in love with them. Raised in the Midwest and California, she and her husband currently share their empty nest with two adorably arrogant cats in the South Carolina Lowcountry where the rich blend of legend, romance, and history fuels her imagination.

Connect with Regan online:
Facebook
Twitter
Instagram

Or follow Regan at:
BookBub
Amazon

For a full list of Regan's books visit Amazon or ReganBlack.com and enjoy excerpts from each of her adrenaline-fueled novels.

ALSO BY REGAN BLACK

Black Ice, Book 4 in Stormwatch, a multi-author series

what she knew, Book 4 in Breakdown, a multi-author series

Guardian Agency/Brotherhood Protectors Series

Unknown Identities Series

Escape Club Heroes, Harlequin Romantic Suspense

The Riley Code, Harlequin Romantic Suspense

Colton Family Saga, Harlequin Romantic Suspense

Knight Traveler Series

The Matchmaker Series

Harlequin Intrigue, written with Debra Webb

Shadows of Justice Series

DON'T MISS

THE EXPLOSIVE SUSPENSE SERIES

A ground-breaking, fast paced 4-book suspense series that will keep you turning pages until the end. Reviews describe BREAKDOWN as "unique," "brilliant" and "the best series of the year." The complete series includes **the dead girl** by Debra Webb, **so many secrets** by Vicki Hinze, **all the lies** by Peggy Webb and **what she knew** by Regan Black. You'll want all four books of the thrilling BREAKDOWN series!

Printed in Great Britain
by Amazon

35548948R00113